eden Hudson

Revenge

of The

Bloodslinger

E. Hudson

Dedication

*This one's for the wizard in the Hawaiian shirt,
the cyborg in the business suit,
and the robot in the socks and sandals.*

E. Hudson

You love it like this,
But what will you do at the end of it?

ONE_

I RODE INTO ARGAMERI UNDER A DARK CURTAIN OF acid rain and parked my Mangshan in a covered alley with a decent view of the dirty little bar where I was meeting the Bloodslinger. Lightning flashed, illuminating the cranes that hung over the City of Thieves like rusty crosses. Pretty fitting omen, considering I was about to talk to a named knight with a Guild record so shiny that she could've used it to light the way home for prodigal sons and daughters everywhere.

I spent a few minutes making sure the Mangshan was positioned out of the way of drips coming through the holes in the alley's awnings. The 'Shan had an acid rain protectant topcoat, but I hated to abuse it. The Mangshan was my baby, a custom-built cobalt and copper crotchrocket, and I treated it right.

With the 'Shan properly protected from the elements, I left the alley and crossed a street that was already under three inches running water. The sewers in this dump were as lackadaisical about their jobs as this city's populace.

Under normal circumstances, you couldn't have paid me to show my face in Argameri. The City of Thieves was a home for the mediocre—second-rate swindlers, underclass drug dealers, and breaker trash. Argameri was a whore uglier and older than her years, despised by everyone but herself, and by herself twice over. Her loyal citizens also happened to have a lifetime bounty on the head of one Jubal D. Van Zandt—dead or alive, but preferably dead—for selling the secret of her secret entrance to the Guild's task force back when they began to crack down on theft and prostitution and all the other fun stuff out there. Apparently, Argameri's citizens had a selective memory when it came to the name of the thief who had emptied the Guild's closest armory and delivered those first-class weapons right into Argamerian hands at only twice the cost of the current surplus market, thereby giving them the ability to defend themselves from said surprise Guild attack well enough to eventually force a negotiation and an armistice.

In spite of their spite, I wasn't worried about being lynched. Man and mutie hadn't made the cell that could hold me yet, and by the time they did, I would be halfway around the world, biting my thumb at them over my shoulder. It was just one of the many things that made me a winner.

The inside of the bar smelled exactly like the outside of the bar looked—dank and dirty. My nose wrinkled in disgust. I don't drink, ever, but if I did, I wouldn't do it in a mudhole like this. The whole place was so poorly ventilated that you could barely hear the rain coming down outside. Might as well inject mildew straight into my veins and cut out the middleman.

Several dirt-encrusted patrons and a barkeeper I strongly suspected of being a gill mutie watched me intentionally step over the soaked doormat, the better to drip on their filthy wood floor. I took off my ventilator and helmet, gave them a grin, and shook the acid rain at their jacket rack.

Sir Carina Xiao, the Bloodslinger, sat in a high-backed booth by a window, watching me through the haze of wrackrath smoke. Even if I hadn't checked her official and unofficial records out in depth before I agreed to meet with her, I would have recognized Carina immediately. She stuck out in Argameri like the proverbial dick in the hotdog bowl—straight back, self-assured movements, clear green eyes, and the dark, flawless skin that came only from the Guild's genetic tampering. You could bet your life sentence that she was sporting hyperfocus, hyperoxygenation, hyperaural, and hypertactile upgrades—and that was just for starters.

"Two-drink minimum," the barkeep gurgled.

"No thanks," I said, shooting him a wink and a finger gun. "I don't make it a habit to drink anything that comes standard with mouth-gonorrhea."

It was hard to tell from this distance and through the smoke, but I was pretty sure I saw Carina smirk at that.

I wove through the bar's haphazard floor plan, set my helmet and ventilator on the table, then slid into the booth across from Carina.

For a split second, the handsome devil in the reflection of my helmet's visor caught my eye. Hair perfect, face blemish-free, stubble under control, easygoing smile that touched my eyes, little scar across the inside of the left eyebrow to show that I had character and draw even more attention to my best feature slash distract from the little bit of slack I can never quite get out of my waistline. Ugly people won't admit this, but life's easier when you're pretty.

I tore my gaze away and pointed at the incensor of wrackrath in front of Carina. "You know that's probably cut with enough mildew to shut down your respiratory system. And even if it's not, there's no way they had fresh grass on hand. It's ten years old if it's a day."

"You're a lot prissier than I expected a thief to be," Carina said.

"Mildew is a very real health concern, Sir Xiao."

"Like mouth-gonorrhea?" Yeah, she was definitely fighting a smile.

Lightning flashed outside our booth's window and illuminated a sinewy pink mass of scar tissue where Carina's left cheek and jaw should have been.

"Holy balls!" I leaned forward to get a better look. "What happened to your face?"

The almost-smile disappeared. "Are you really Jubal Van Zandt? Because I was under the impression that I would be dealing with a professional."

"Hey, I don't set up meetings with you and then criticize the way you conduct them. I saw something that surprised me and I asked about it. Beats pretending like I don't notice that half of your face is melted off."

"They're acid scars," she said.

"Gross," I said.

That reaction didn't seem to offend her as much as my alleged lack of professionalism.

"Are you even going to ask me about the contract?" she asked.

"Once we get the preliminaries out of the way."

"Which are?"

"How the shit did that happen to your face?" I asked. "Additionally, what's a good, God-fearing knight of the Guild doing hiring the best thief in the history of the Revived Earth? Specifically, a thief her superiors banned all Guild contact with."

Carina was quiet for so long that I thought she wasn't going to answer either question. Then she ran her thumb over the burner of the incensor, wiping at a water stain. "I have to get into a place that can't be accessed. You did a job last year, broke into The Hotel and got away untouched with Crangel's Sledgehammer in tow. The place I'm going is locked up tighter."

"Hmm." Tighter than an ultimate-security prison? Energy zinged and zanged up and down my arms and legs at the thought. I shifted from one side of my butt to the other, then shook my shoulders out. "Intriguing. Very intriguing indeed. Especially considering that Guild policy is to blast or smash their way into any place that won't open its doors willingly." I locked onto her bright green eyes. "A knight—a named knight from a Guild family older than Emden itself, no less—should be able to put in a work order for a couple thousand troops and shoot her way in, shouldn't she?"

Carina didn't break eye contact or show any outward hesitation at what she was about to say. "This job is unsanctioned. It violates Guild law, and I want to keep it off the books."

"Boy, have you come to the right thief, sister." I leaned in closer. "Which law are we breaking?"

"Vengeance belongs to the Lord," she said.

Normally, I don't ask for my clients' life stories because I don't care about their crazy stupid boring lives. Boring people love to tell you why they're all hot and bothered to get their hands on this-and-such an object or into that-and-such a place. Interesting people, the really interesting ones, don't want to tell you anything. You've got to pry them open like giant oysterlusks.

"Who are we getting revenge on?" I asked.

"Witches. Aguas brujahs, based in Soam now."

"Neat, a plane ride." I sat forward and leaned my elbows on the table. "I'll need to be flown first class, obviously. Make a note of it. What did these brujahs do?"

"Murder."

"To whom?"

"A Guild knight."

"Your boyfriend?"

"My mentor, advisor, direct superior, and father."

"So, what you're saying is you don't have a boyfriend," I said.

Carina's non-acid-scarred jaw ticked. "They used craft to seduce my father, poison his mind, then destroy him from the inside out."

"Smells like somebody didn't want a step-mommy." I did some calculations based on the Guild's file on Carina. "What's it been, like, twenty years since Mommy died in the crusades? That's a long time to have Daddy all to yourself."

"This has nothing to do with jealousy." Carina's eyes flashed green fire. "I understand that no one wants to spend their life alone, and I wouldn't have begrudged my father a helpmate. Not if she had come to him without ulterior motives."

"Probably would've gone a long way to alleviate your concerns if she'd been a Jesusfreak like you and your Guild buddies, too, huh?"

"At first, she pretended to be." Carina's voice had almost softened when she said that. My ears perked up at the almost-sound of it.

"She played on somebody's sympathies," I said.

"She came to the Guild as a new follower, supposedly a convert from the Soam missionaries. My father had a past with the area, spoke her language. He wanted to help her grow in Christ."

"Not as much as she wanted to help him grow in his pants. She was smoking hot, wasn't she?"

Carina chose to ignore that remark. "We didn't find out until much later that the aid group who'd been assigned to her village's area was dead."

"So you're assuming she killed your missionary buddies, too."

"The official causes of death were drowning," Carina said. "But all of them? No one stayed on land while the rest of the group was swimming? One of the drowned aid workers was well known among friends for being unable to swim and terrified of deep water. But the Guild won't prosecute foreign parties on circumstantial evidence."

"Pretty stupid," I said as if I was on her side. "What about in the case of your father? Do you know that these brujahs killed him or are you just assuming they did because he drowned?"

"His official cause of death was suicide," Carina said. "But it was the brujah. She drove my father away from God, used him to spy on the Guild, and by the time he realized how far gone he was, there wasn't any way to get back. Before he did any more damage, he ended it."

"I see. Took the ol' noble gut-cutting way out. Bet that was a messy cleanup. So, where do I come in and what's the plan as you see it?"

"The brujahs returned to Soam, which is where they're most powerful and best protected. I can't even find their village without already knowing where it is. It's under some kind of paradoxical magic lockdown."

"Sounds like one of the ancient epics."

She raised an eyebrow at that. "You're familiar with the Potter legends?"

"Look, I understand that your prejudices about thieves run deep—you set up a meeting in this nasty little mudhole in Argameri for fuck's sake—but you're not working with some run-of-the-river breaker whose biggest payday was that time he pawned three screens in one night." I tapped my chest. "I'm Jubal fucking Van Zandt. I picked my first axolotl lock when I was six. I untied the Jordanian knot when I was nine. I am the only living being—human or mutie—to have gotten into and out of The Hotel without Crangel's express permission, and I did it all without focus chems or magic. I've got a loft in Taern, a summer place overlooking the Crystal Lakes, and a standing penthouse reservation at every five-star in Emden. I'm not only literate, but I make it my business to know all the First Earth epics, legends, and lore. I am the best damned thief in the history of the Revived Earth, sister, and honestly, based on what I've seen from you so far,

I'm starting to doubt whether you're prepared to pay my fee."

A dressing-down like that is usually enough to embarrass a strong-willed client and give me the upper hand in negotiations. Carina just nodded.

"Good," she said. "Because I'm not interested in hiring some illiterate breaker trash who'll slit my throat when his supply of ember dust runs out. I need the best, and believe it or not, I'm willing to pay for the best."

I clapped my hands together. "Then let's get started. How did you hear about me?"

"Guild files. Their records on you are full of suspicions, first-person accounts, and rumors. No arrests, no charges, and no incriminating evidence that you didn't purposely leave behind for someone to find. I investigated Laars Gonzalez's allegations that—"

Carina broke off, pulling a well-worn knuckgun from inside her leather jacket and pointing it at the two big guys approaching our booth.

"Don't take another step," she said. "Drop your weapons."

They stopped, but didn't drop the rust-caked knife or the stunclub.

"Uh-oh," I said. "Looks like somebody recognized me. I'll sign one autograph apiece, guys, but then I've really got to get back to work."

The bigger of the two, who looked like he dogfought for funsies on the weekends, growled, "The Guild has no jurisdiction here, knight. The man you're associating with is a wanted fugitive in Argameri."

"That's true," I told Carina. "Dead or alive. The bounty's huge."

She didn't take her eyes off the bruisers as she asked me, "Why didn't you say something when I suggested meeting here?"

"Aw, come on, look at these guys! They couldn't take a cucumber from a slime whore. Besides, I wanted to see what you'd do. Shoot 'em and let's get back to business."

"What are you wanted for?" she asked.

"For being better than them. They're jealous that I sold them out before they could think of a way to do it to me."

The second guy, whose face was covered in fishhook tattoos, pointed his snapping and sparking stunclub at me. "Your betrayal cost hundreds of Argamerian lives!"

"Really?" I said. "Because I heard it was thousands."

Apparently, Tattoo-Face wasn't going to stand for me correcting him. He let out an ear-hair-curling scream and lunged at me. Dogfight guy went off at the same time, stabbing his knife at Carina.

I didn't stick around to find out what happened. I'm a lover, not a fighter. I slipped under the table where I would be safe from any ricochets and blunt-force trauma. But not from dust wads. The little buggers clung to my pants, smearing their nasty coatings of skin cells and dried mucus so deep into the weave that I would never get the viruses out.

"This city is disgusting." I tried to slap and swipe my pants clean. "I hope all of your children die screaming."

On the other side of the table, the knuckgun went off. Tattoo-Face wailed, and the stunclub bounced to the floor and rolled away.

Carina's legs lunged out from under the table. A second later, she and Dogfight guy hit the floor, her with one fist clamped around his knife-hand. They rolled around like that, then Carina cocked back the knuckgun and jabbed Dogfight just under the sternum with the muzzle. The air woofed out of him, and she wrenched the knife away easily.

Tattoo-Face's legs took a step toward Carina, but she rolled up to her knees so that I could only see her back, and reached up toward him. Her knuckgun's chain-driven saw clicked on, assaulting our eardrums with its air-vibrating whine.

"I'm done!" Tattoo-Face yelled. "I'm done! I give!"

"Drop it," Carina said.

The stunclub hit the floor and rolled away for a second time.

I wriggled out from under the table so I could see better. Carina was holding the saw edge of her knuckgun's handguard so close to Tattoo-Face's crotch that an accidental twitch would vasectomize him.

"Whatever you do, don't sneeze," I told him. Then I reached down and wiped a handful of the dust off my ruined pants and smeared it across the underside of his nose.

Tattoo-Face opened his mouth to yell something undoubtedly derogatory at me, but immediately got a snout-full of dust. His eyes squeezed shut. His chest hitched.

"Fight it," I said. "Think of your unborn children."

"Out the door, Van Zandt," Carina said. She stood up and thumbed off the knuckgun's saw, removing the danger from Tattoo-Face's balls the second before he sneezed so hard his brain would've exploded out his ears if he'd had one.

I grabbed my helmet and ventilator off the table and stepped over Dogfight. His face was nearly purple. Didn't look like he'd reached the point yet where you can finally take a breath after getting the wind knocked out of you. Tattoo-Face wasn't faring much better. Blood dripped off the fingertips of his left hand, and from his elbow down, his arm was white and shaking.

As Carina and I backed away, she stuck the knife in her belt and picked up the stunclub. Neither Tattoo-Face nor Dogfight looked to be in any shape to go after their weapons, but I can appreciate the better-safe-than-sorry attitude. Especially when it's saving my skin.

OUTSIDE, CARINA TOSSED THE KNIFE AND stunclub into the rushing water of the gutter.

"You should've said something cool," I told her as we crossed the street.

Her eyebrows came together in confusion. "Something cool?"

We turned into the alley where I'd stashed the 'Shan. The downpour had died off a little, but I still had to raise my voice so Carina could hear me over the hiss and tick of the droplets on the rusty awning.

"Yeah, after you kicked their asses," I said. "Like, 'Maybe you can turn in what's left of your dignity for the bounty.' That's not a great example, but you get the idea."

"That's gloating," she said. "It's bad form."

I rolled my eyes. "I bet you're gallons of fun to hang out with. You know what? For the duration of this job, I'll take care of the saying cool shit. I won't even charge extra. Maybe you'll learn something."

"I already learned that mouth-gonorrhea is a very real health concern." She said it with a straight face, but her tone lilted upward just enough to give her away.

"Mildew, too," I said, slinging one leg over the Mangshan and popping up the kickstand. "You really ought to wear a ventilator in the city."

Carina nodded, but not as if she was conceding that I was right. "That's what people tell me. What's our next step?"

"Next I put out the ol' whiskers and catfish around," I said. "I'll call you when I've got a bite."

In reality, the process wasn't that catch-all-and-sift. I had some ideas on where I would start, but it was best to keep the preparation stage sounding mysterious. Clients don't want to think they're paying to see whether my hunches will pay off, they want to think they're paying for time-consuming legwork and research.

"Now," I said, leaning on the handlebars, "Let's get down to the nitty-gritty—money. You'll need to set up an incidentals account in my name with...oh, eight or ten thousand should cover my dailies for the duration of the job. My fee is a separate figure, and it will need to be transferred directly into my personal account. Then we'll get this showboat on the river."

Her eyebrow cocked, redirecting a raindrop from her widow's peak, down her forehead toward her straight, dark nose. "You haven't done anything yet."

"I don't use the Guild's honor system," I said. "My motto is ass, grass, or cash up front—and you'll want to keep in mind that I don't accept those first two as valid forms of payment. The minute the transfer goes through to my bank account, I start looking for leads on your aguas brujahs. Not before."

"How much?"

"For anybody else, seven hundred thousand." I shot her with a finger gun. "For you, nine."

"I'll pay you half up front, half upon completion."

"That's not how this works, sister. You want off-the-books work, you pay off-the-books payment plans."

I thought she was going to push the issue, but she didn't. That made me nervous.

"Give me your number," she said.

I did.

She messed around on her wristpiece for a few seconds, then looked up. "Nine hundred thousand will be in your account when they start the automated transfers in the morning."

"Soon as it is, we're in business," I said.

She stretched her hand out and I shook. I was about to pull my hand back, but she didn't let go.

"Van Zandt?" She looked into my pupils like she was trying to catalogue the rods and cones along the back of my eyes. "There's a dead man's switch on the transfer."

Which meant the Guild had more in their files on me than just what they suspected me of having stolen. I grinned.

"Better do your best not to die, then," I said, squeezing her hand tighter. "If that money gets repoed, I'm going after the next closest person to you. I don't work for free."

The Bloodslinger didn't say anything to that, just held my hand a moment longer, then let it go.

TWO_

S INCE I WAS ALREADY IN THE NEIGHBORHOOD— figuratively speaking—I drove up to the City at the Pass and checked into the Sharp Right Turn under my standing reservation as the esteemed J.D. Vance. The storm hadn't totally moved on, and I didn't want to make the whole run back to Taern in a downpour. Besides, I could do my hunch-checking tomorrow while enjoying the Sharp Right Turn's five-star breakfast as easily as I could anywhere else.

The entirety of the City at the Pass had been carved into the rock of the mountainside back when the Revived Earth was still reviving, so the single entry point into and through was a narrow two-lane. Easily defensible, terrible for traffic. I was still eight miles out when the stop-and-go started stopping and going. I took my feet off the pegs and skated my sneaks along the pavement to support the 'Shan.

Some fishshit-stupid adrenaddict on a much cheaper crotchrocket shot past me toward the city's entry, weaving in and out of traffic like a goon. Long dark hair streaked with bright blue whipped around the back of her helmet like a fly-fishing lure. My thumb traced the throttle and my bones hummed inside my body, but I had the self-control to stay put. I watched her disappear into the gridlock and wished her roadrash to match the brain damage she was going to have when someone in a much larger vehicle scraped her across the asphalt.

As I was watching, the adrenaddict reared up onto her fat back tire and wheelied down the slick center stripe. Crying shame, wasting a body that looked that good in leather on a brain like that.

"This is why you can't have nice things," I told her. "Or live to see old age."

Imagine my not-surprise when I pulled through the carved mountain-rock pillars of the Sharp Right Turn's parking garage an hour later and found her cheap-ass Jasper parked in the moto section. I knew it was hers because there was a wide swipe of skidrash across the tank and the peg on that side had been ground down from sliding.

I'd been planning to go straight up to J.D. Vance's penthouse and order some room service, but once I saw the Jasper sitting there, I knew where its driver would be. She'd made it to the hotel alive, so she needed to celebrate. The minibar in her room wouldn't be loud and annoying enough for someone like her, so she would be at the nightclub on the Sharp Right Turn's balcony.

So I checked in, almost sent the only baggage I'd brought with me—my helmet and ventilator—up to the rooms with a bellhop, then changed my mind. She wouldn't have taken the time or consideration to send her gear up to her room. She would've headed straight for the club.

I headed straight for the club, too, helmet and ventilator in hand, grinning like an addict on an adrenaline high.

It took all of two seconds to spot her blue-streaked hair. Her helmet and ventilator were lying on the bar, forgotten, while she did flaming scall shots at the center of half a dozen hooping and hollering admirers. She was probably going to nail all of them at one point or another tonight.

I ordered a coffee—the great thing about the Sharp Right Turn is that it stocks only real coffee straight from the Old Castle, none of that fake chicory stuff, so you don't even have to specify when you order—and watched her from a table at the railing. I could've looked out into the growing darkness and watched the streetlights pop on down in the city below, illuminating little bulbs of nearly-rain mist, but if you've seen night falling on one city carved into a mountainside, you've seen night falling on them all.

The adrenaddict wouldn't come to me, not while she had a captive audience, so I decided to get some practice before I went after her.

There are all sorts of books and articles out there that anyone with a reader or a reader app can—and frequently do—access to learn how to pick up women. Those books are all targeted at the same sort of gullible loser who also buys unfiltered water because the hippies say it's good for their immune system. The truth is, picking up women is a numbers game. No matter how handsome, charming, or rich you are, for every nine women you start a conversation with, one will agree to go to your room. In fact, one is waiting for somebody to ask her to go to their room. The thing those losers reading the How-To books are so scared of—the thing they buy those damn books to learn how to avoid—is getting rejected by the other eight.

I got the first rejection out of the way fast. Leaned toward the redhead at the table across from mine and said, "Hey, babe, want to go upstairs and blow me?"

The redhead giggled like she couldn't believe she'd heard me right, then went back to talking with her friends.

"What about you?" I pointed at her fat friend. "You look like you've got something super-antibiotics can't cure. Want to sexually transmit it to me?"

"Och, fuck off."

I turned to the quiet blonde with them. She didn't look comfortable at all in this crowd, probably insecure because of her big honkin' nose.

"All right, ugly duckling," I said. "I guess it's me and you."

The blonde sucked into herself like a mouse hiding in its hole, but the fat chick stepped up again.

"Ah said fuck off," she snapped. "Ah'll go get the security guy."

I had to set my coffee down so I wouldn't spill it from laughing too hard.

Instead of going for SRT Security, they found a table on the other side of the room, away from the open air.

Three rejections down. Time to get serious.

I picked up my coffee and approached a standing table near the center of the club. The woman there was alone, scanning the faces.

"You weren't looking for me, were you?" I asked, turning on the shy-but-trying-to-come-out-of-my-shell expression.

Like most people, her instinct was to make the introvert feel safe and welcome. She gave me a smile. "Maybe I was."

I laughed in a self-deprecating way and turned my chin down a little to communicate that I was incapable of thinking of myself as any better than the common ass-ugly mutie.

"He's tall, dark, and handsome, isn't he? The guy you were actually looking for," I said. For the record, I am all of those things and more. I shrugged. "It's okay, you can admit it."

She smiled wider and bobbed her head back and forth in a gesture of *Okay, you got me.* "Well, maybe. But then I met this other good-looking fellow who seemed like he might be fun to hang out with."

Hang out with was code for *Never have sex with.* Rejection disguised as a compliment.

I talked to her for a while longer just to see what kinds of conversational holes I could back her into. When my coffee ran out, I told her I'd be right back and headed for the bar. I wasn't coming back.

Honestly, I was growing bored with the whole enterprise—people are way too easy to manipulate— but I still had to rack up four more losses and a win, so I pressed on.

I got rejections five and six out of the way while I was waiting for the bartender to brew me some fresh coffee, by first propositioning a woman who was obviously on a date, then by propositioning the man who had been whispering in her ear. Then I tried to talk up a guy who was trying desperately to pick up any woman at all. I don't actually swing that way, but allowing yourself to fall into patterns based on your preferences is the fastest way to lead authorities straight to your front door. It's best to mix things up now and then, keep people guessing.

The adrenaddict was still at the bar, surrounded by her posse of overly loud admirers. Even after all the time and booze they'd wasted, none of those goons had gotten up the courage to seal the deal. I pushed through to where one was doing a belly shot off of her exposed midriff.

I took her hand and pulled her up to sitting, scattering salt crystals onto her lap.

"Hey!" yelled the goon who'd just finished his shot.

"You're the one who rode in on the algae-green Jasper?" I asked the adrenaddict. This close, her face looked soft and ethereal against her hair.

Her perfect eyebrows crinkled. "Yeah. Is something wrong? I stuck my parking ticket to the tank when I parked. It should still be there. I've got the stub."

"Nothing's wrong." I held up my helmet and ventilator. "I parked beside you and noticed your skidrash. Take a bad slide?"

She grinned. Nothing adrenaddicts like more than telling war stories. "Some slug in a hot rod wasn't looking where he was going, knocked me right between the wheels of a cargo carrier. I was in traction for a month, but my Jassie barely had a mark on her."

Sure, if you didn't count those gigantic screaming scratches down the side.

I rolled my eyes like the wreck wasn't entirely her fault for being a fishshit moron and fucking around in the first place. She'd probably been driving with her eyes shut or something equally stupid.

"Siltbrains think because they're in a car or truck they own the road," I said. "I had a close call the other day with my 'Shan."

"'Shan?" she asked, hazel eyes turning dark and hungry. "As in Mangshan?"

I nodded. "Seven series."

"Seven? I've never seen a seven series in person." She slid off the bar and grabbed her gear. "Can we?"

It would be way too easy to be a serial killer.

THE ADRENADDICT CIRCLED THE 'SHAN LIKE SHE actually knew what she was looking at. "This thing is so virgin. Are you sure you rode it in?"

"Yeah," I said. *This is what a bike looks like when you don't fuck it up showboating.* "I keep its regular detailing appointments."

"Man, so would I if I had something this nice."

She wouldn't.

The adrenaddict trailed her fingers across the 'Shan's grips. Disgust bloomed in my stomach, but I kept the self-satisfied smirk she would expect to see from another member of her species on my face.

She turned back to me, a quirk in her full lips. "Can we take it out?"

"Nah, it's still misting. I don't take it out in the acid rain if I can help it."

She smiled and leaned back on the 'Shan's seat, one hand on the handlebars, one on the rear fender in a practiced pose that pushed up her breasts while making her creamy stomach look flat and inviting. I admired the slice of heaven peeking out at the bottom of her shirt. I've got a thing for women's tummies, and hers was exquisite—velvety café au lait skin, with one dark freckle just below her navel.

"Maybe it won't be raining in an hour or two," she said. "We could go upstairs for a while."

That skin, those curves, that face—all absolutely wasted on that cream cheese she called a brain.

I shook my head. "Nah, I don't nail fat chicks."

The sultry smile faded away as what I'd said sank through her thick skull. "Fat? Fuck you, I'm not fat. I'm a size one!"

"In Soam, maybe. Get off my ride before you bend the kickstand."

The adrenaddict screeched at me. She didn't have the mental capacity to come up with a real response. Probably one too many concussions.

"I'm serious," I said. "Get off. Mangshans are custom built, and I don't want to spend a couple thousand bucks replacing parts because you're too dumb to follow simple instructions."

"Asshole!" she squawked, coming off the seat like she'd been ejected. "I was on the cover of the last *Motogirls!*"

"And I bet the fat-fondlers thought you were very sexy."

She gave another high-octave shriek, then turned on the ground-down heel of her motorcycle boot. Her leather-clad ass had just the right amount of jiggle when she stomped. I grinned as I watched it go.

Halfway to the hotel's parking garage entrance, she turned back and yelled, "Like you're such a fucking catch! You're the blubber-ass!"

"Sour grapes," I called.

She screeched again and slammed her helmet against a mountain-rock pillar as she passed.

I giggled. Once she got into the elevator headed upstairs, I fired up the 'Shan and moved it down a couple levels in the garage, then took the slipcover off of another bike and slid it onto mine. Wouldn't want some crazy adrenaddict coming back later with a screwdriver and taking revenge, now would we?

I checked my wristpiece on my way to the elevators.

"Would you look at the time." I chuckled and shook my head. "And me with work tomorrow!"

THE BLOODSLINGER'S MONEY POPPED UP IN MY account at exactly one minute past seven the next morning. My wristpiece beeped with the notification the second it came through. I got up, showered, and had a leisurely breakfast in J.D. Vance's penthouse while I did some cursory research and called around. My hunch was right on. All in all, it took me nineteen minutes to find a contact and set up a meeting, but I let Carina stew the rest of the day so she would feel like she was getting her money's worth. I took the scenic drive back to Taern so I would be closer to her beloved Guild, then messaged her just before I went to sleep.

THREE_

CARINA LOOKED AROUND THE DARK INTERIOR OF the diner before sweeping a crumpled straw wrapper off her seat and sliding in across the table from me. "You were mad at me for stereotyping, and not two days later you pick this dive?"

"Normally, I wouldn't be caught dead eating in any place with fewer than four Sarlean stars," I admitted. "But I had to meet up with someone here once, and it turns out their line cook is a fucking magician with biscuits and gravy. Don't bother with that." She'd been pulling the little menu card out of the holder. "I already ordered for us. You can thank me after you try them."

"Do they even serve breakfast this late?"

I shrugged. "It's six a.m. somewhere."

When the waitress came by again, Carina ordered a glass of filtered water even though I advised against it. They might have the best biscuits and gravy in the country, but I'd seen what passed for filtered water in this place.

A few minutes later, Carina's water showed up looking like it had been filtered through an old jizz sock.

"You're going to die someday," I said, shrugging. "Might as well be today."

The good side of Carina's mouth smirked. "I'll survive. I've got an iron stomach."

"I bet that makes it tough to swim," I said.

"You learn to compensate." She took a drink and didn't even grimace. "So, what did you find out?"

"I found our starting point, that's what. You're going to need two first-class seats on an airliner to Nytundi." I gestured at her wristpiece. "You're welcome to start booking while we talk, although I doubt the tickets are in high demand, what with the war going on."

"Wait, Nytundi?" Carina leaned forward, elbows on the table. "How do brujahs from Soam have anything to do with a little island nation halfway across the world?"

"Everything has to do with everything," I said. "That's the first thing you learn in my business. It's all part of the same knot. The second thing you learn is, if you're looking for an in with murderers, you go to the murder capital of the Revived Earth."

"So we can become statistics."

I waved my hand at that. "Tourists almost never disappear there anymore."

The waitress dropped off the plates, and I went to work on mine. Carina ruined hers by adding red pepper flakes before she even tried a bite, but I politely refrained from calling her a tasteless retard because it's rude to talk with your mouth full.

When we were done, Carina wiped her mouth with a napkin and leaned back in the booth.

"I ate entirely too much," she said. "I can't believe you were able to get through two orders."

I patted my stomach like I didn't give any fucks about what she was implying. "It takes a lot to fuel this finely-tuned love machine. Besides, I didn't hear you complaining while you were chowing down."

"They were good," she said, shrugging.

"Maybe you should consider eating out more often. If you had some halfway feminine curves, people might not focus so much on the messed-up side of your face."

She rolled her eyes and started working on her wristpiece. "How soon can you be ready to leave?"

"Ten minutes from now."

"Looks like the soonest flight leaves tomorrow. I'll message you the ticket information. Meet you at the airport?"

"As long as the seats are first class. If they're not, I'll complain the whole way to Nytundi and fill your life with misery and woe."

FOUR_

"THIS IS…" CARINA STARED AROUND HER AT the plane's first-class cabin. "…wasteful… extravagant… It's overly luxurious, to a ridiculous level."

"The word you're looking for is mediocre," I said, leaning my seat back as far as it would go. "When I was a kid, these things folded out into beds. Now look at them. And the carpet? See, this is the problem with economic progress. The underclasses start thinking they've got the right to fly too, so the air travel companies start catering to their shit tastes and shit wages, downgrading everything, and the people who actually have the money to fly in the fashion a human being should fly are the ones who end up losing."

"Do you ever stop and listen to the things you're saying?"

"Not if I can help it." I laced my hands behind my head and wiggled my shoulders, trying to get comfortable. "Why don't you relax? It's a long way to Nytundi."

"You confirmed the meeting with our contact?" Carina asked.

"Asking questions like that is the opposite of relaxing."

"Did you?"

"Yes."

"And you're sure the information's good?"

"Good as you're going to get."

Carina put her elbows on the armrests and leaned her head back against her seat. Probably as comfortable as Guild knights ever got. Those goons had a real problem with the luxuries of this world. Really putting all their eggs in the glorious afterlife basket.

"Why the Guild?" I asked.

She rolled her head my way. "What are you talking about?"

"I get that your family's been part of the Guild for almost as long as the Guild has existed. But you're obviously okay with thinking for yourself or we wouldn't be on this plane right now. You could have chosen to do something else with your life. Strike out on your own. Be someone. Why blindly follow the Guild?"

For a long time Carina was silent, her expression turned inward, but I was starting to get the hang of her rhythms. This was something she did before she just started talking: she thought.

That meant a lot of really interesting things. For one, it meant that she'd grown up in an environment that encouraged coherent answers. It also meant that the people who expected those answers had been willing to wait for them. Wrong answers must've been punishable by something the younger Carina had hated or been afraid of, and so she took the time to come up with the right answers. I wondered what the punishment had been and whether her father had been the one to dole it out. Probably not, considering she was so thirsty to avenge the guy's death.

"It's not blind following," she said finally. "I've seen the Guild inside and out, from every angle. It's not always pretty, and it's not always perfect, but the people who commit their lives to it are really trying to do what's right."

"What's right according to God," I added.

Carina shrugged. "Yeah."

"How do you know God's right?"

"He hasn't failed me yet," she said. "Based on His track record, I have faith that He won't."

"Except in the matter of avenging your old man."

"The Guild failed in that, not God."

I threw up my hands. "See! You're not some mindless sheep. You could've done something with your life besides holy wars and inquisitions and whatever else you meatheads do for fun."

"Shaming sinners," she volunteered, the unscarred corner of her mouth lifting. "That's actually our most popular intramural sport."

☰

"THE ELECTRICITY IS ABOUT TO GO OUT," a feminine voice whispered in my ear.

I sat up, heart pounding.

My flame kigao was floating just above Carina's seat, the reds and oranges of burning impurities roiling and boiling in the shape of an unclothed, barely-developed pubescent girl, almost bent into what a kigao might consider a sitting position, if indeed kigaoe could consider anything at all.

Most of the other first-class passengers were sleeping, but the few who were awake didn't seem distressed. No screams, no panic, nothing obviously out of place. A steward sidled past, the blankets he was carrying whispering through the kigao's flaming hair undamaged.

The kigao patted my hand gently and blinked sympathetic eyes the color of burning blood. "The electricity is about to go out."

It damn sure didn't look like anything was wrong, but the kigao had never steered me wrong before.

Carina came down the aisle from the bathroom. She and the steward said the appropriate excuse mes and squeezed past one another on her way back to her seat.

"The electricity is about to go out," the kigao said.

"Yeah, yeah," I mumbled.

"Yeah what?" Carina asked, sitting down in the middle of the kigao.

For a second their forms overlapped and it looked like Carina was on fire. Her dark skin shined through the flames like cooling lava, and her eyes seemed to be on the verge of exploding into fountains of blood-soaked emerald starlight. Then the kigao stood and flitted off to stand half in and half out of the plane's wall.

"Nothing," I said. "Do you notice anything…weird?"

"The electricity is about to go out," the kigao said helpfully.

Carina straightened up in her seat and turned her head, scanning the interior of the first-class cabin for threats. "I don't think so. What exactly am I looking for?"

I slouched and shook my head. "I don't know. Never mind."

The kigao touched my shoulder. "The electricity—"

I shrugged her hand off. "I heard you, damn it!"

"Van Zandt, are you all right?"

"Yeah, just peachy. Something's about to blow up in our faces, that's all."

"What?"

I rolled my eyes. "Who fucking knows? Maybe the whole damn plane." I slammed open my window shade. The kigao flickered out of my way so I could look out. "Are we still over the Crist? We're more likely to survive if we crash down in water, right?"

"If you know something, now would be the time to tell me," Carina said. "I can't help if I don't know what we're facing."

"Or maybe it won't happen until we land. Sometimes it takes a while, but the way she phrases it always—"

"She? Are you on something?"

"I don't take chems!" I smacked my window shade shut again. Black treble hooks of restless, crawling energy twisted inside my skin. I slumped back in my seat, rubbed my hands across my face, and joggled my legs. "Did the power ever go out when you were growing up? You lived in the Guild's fortress, right? Did the electricity ever go out or was it steady enough in Taern back then that it was always on?"

Carina nodded slowly. "It went out sometimes. Usually during the megacell storms."

"At night?"

"Sometimes."

"Hmm. Hmm, hmm, hmm." I ran my hand through my hair. Sweat prickled down my back and trickled into my asscrack. I couldn't sit still any longer, so I stood up and pushed past Carina to the aisle.

At the same time, the curtain separating the first-class cabins from the rest of the passengers flew back and a skinny Nytundi teenager shoved through, waving a FATrifle half his height and probably twice his weight. The kid opened his mouth to yell something.

"Oh, that's just great!" I interrupted, gesturing at him. "This asshole. Let me guess, buddy—you're taking this plane for your side in the ongoing Nytundi hostilities?"

The kid didn't answer, so I switched to Nytundi's New Tongue.

"Hijacking? Really? In the middle of the fucking week? I vouched for your stupid country, kid. That'll teach me. Never vouch for anything."

"Sit in your seat!" The kid bumblefucked up the Anglish so bad even I almost couldn't understand him. He pointed the FATrifle at me. "Sit down! Do not move! I will shoot!"

"Could you at least enunciate? I mean, shit, you're the mouthpiece for this operation? What is it, a suicide run? Your friends couldn't stand your stuttering anymore, so they sent you to crash the plane into— Wait, does Nytundi even have buildings, or is it all just mud huts?"

"Shut your fucking mouth or I'll put a bullet in your head!" the kid screeched in his native language.

"I'll believe it when I see it, you cross-eyed little piece of fugu shit," I said.

Carina slipped past me like a cold breeze. The kid swung the muzzle of the FAT her way, but she was already on him. One malnourished child suicide soldier wasn't even close to a match for a Guild knight. She grabbed the rifle and jerked it out of his hands. The strap of the FAT yanked him forward. Carina slammed the rifle butt into his stomach, then smashed her fist down on the back of his head when he doubled over. He dropped like a bag of rickets and calcium deficiency.

Then Carina swung the FAT around, tucked the butt up against her shoulder, and headed through the curtain and toward the back of the plane.

"Drop your weapons!" she yelled.

I ran back to the curtain and swiped it aside. If Carina got killed in an in-air dispute on this job, I was out my fee plus the return ticket.

Luckily, the kid's hijack-mates were as outclassed as he had been. Carina had the other three on the floor and secured in about ten seconds.

Which turned out to be inversely proportional to the amount of time the stewards and stewardesses spent fawning over her afterward. It wasn't like she was some untrained, unexpected hero. Carina killed bad guys for a living—had been doing so since she was a kid, as Guild knights were wont to do. Even she looked uncomfortable with the weird amounts of admiration these siltbrained morons were heaping on her.

"For fuck's sake, it's not like she saved the Revived Earth or something," I snapped at them. "Don't you people have other passengers to steward? Pull your lips off of her ass so she can sit down already."

They all took turns at giving me their hairiest nictitating membrane as they stalked off.

"That's right, hate the guy who suggests you do your job." I sat back in my seat and kicked up the footrest. "God forbid you be forced to earn your paycheck."

Carina sat down next to me, trying unsuccessfully to fight off a grin. "Making friends, everywhere you go."

I shot a wink and a finger gun at a stewardess who was dragging her feet. She bit her thumb at me before spinning around and stalking off down the aisle.

Then I realized what had happened. I threw my hands up. "You didn't say anything cool! Neither of us did. We're sustaining a severe pithiness deficit on this mission."

That made Carina laugh out loud. I don't know who the sound surprised more, her or me. She pressed her fingers to her lips and stopped herself as soon as the first syllable escaped her throat.

For a long time we sat there not talking. Carina scratched the back of her head, then picked at a thread on her armrest.

"Your hand is shaking," I said. "Actually, all of you is shaking. You weren't scared of those kids, were you?"

"No, I was scared of the .50 caliber grapeshot they had loaded."

I threw back my head and laughed until my eyes watered and my stomach hurt.

When I finally calmed down some, Carina got serious. "Before this all went down, you said something about what *she* said, but the hostiles I found were all male. From what I've read, it's really uncommon for any Nytundi woman to join the military or guerilla forces. It goes against their cultural psychology. Did a civilian tell you something or did you overhear some women talking about one of these guys carrying a weapon? If there's someone else on the plane who might be involved, I need to know."

"You stopped the imminent threat," I said. "There's no one else involved that I know of. There's nothing else to worry about. Yet. I'll let you know if something else comes up."

"You were really freaked out, Van Zandt." Her dark eyebrows pulled low over her green eyes. "When I first came back from the bathroom, you looked like you were about to vomit seawater. If I didn't know any better, I would almost say the second you saw that kid with the rifle, you were relieved."

"I *was* relieved," I said. "I was relieved our whole damn plane wasn't about to take us on an impromptu tour of the ocean floor. Anyway, you're really sweaty now. You should see if your new fan club has anything you can borrow to towel off with. You look disgusting."

Carina leaned her seat back. She closed her eyes, but her breathing didn't change. She wasn't asleep.

"Don't you care that you look like something a kraken digested?" I asked.

She shrugged without opening her eyes.

I chewed on my thumbnail for a while.

"What was your dad like?" I asked her.

Carina looked at me. "Why?"

"Why what? I'm trying to make small talk."

A long pause followed while she stared at me, but it didn't feel the same as when she was thinking carefully before responding. This time I got the uncomfortable feeling that she was trying to figure me out.

"Never mind," I said. "Go back to sleep."

I shut off my overhead light and laid my seat back again.

After a while, Carina shut her light off, too. In the half-light, I could see her turn on her side as if she were lying in bed next to me.

I was starting to wonder whether she actually had fallen asleep when she said in a really small, quiet voice, "He was the best."

FIVE_

THE WAR IN NYTUNDI ISN'T OFFICIALLY A WAR. It's more of a stalemate between the two main political factions, with some executions, suicide bombings, guerilla attacks, and rude name-calling going on behind the scenes. But the Nytundi government is always pretty sure that they're doing a good job keeping the whole affair under wraps, which is why Carina, I, and all of the other passengers aboard Flight 1751 from Emden were allowed to land and walk around unescorted in what passed for a capital city on this floater of an island.

Of course, we and pretty much every other foreigner stuck out like the noose in the rosary pile. Nytundians were your classic third world inhabitants— no genetic modifications, no plasties, outdated technology, overchemmed and undernourished. Even their superrich—who I assume could afford payments on both the bombed-out shell of what used to be a tarpaper shack *and* a pair of shoes—were little skinny stick people with hair like dried straw and skin the color of a catfish's belly. It was gross.

The only good thing about Nytundi was that everything a foreigner could possibly be looking for was located in its capital city so you didn't have to run around the island on wild goose chases. The capital was divided up into districts by the seven rivers that flowed to The Waters at the city center. To meet our contact, we had to cross the rolling log bridges that spanned the rivers between the business district, the tourist district, and the hotel and *sarai* district.

When we got to the first bridge, Carina stood back and watched a few of the locals cross. The unevenly spaced logs dipped underwater, rolled, and spun. Tourists laughed and screeched and tried to take pictures with their wristpieces as the logs sunk beneath their feet and their shoes filled with what looked like pure radioactive sewage. The locals ignored the tourists, hopping and skipping across the logs without hesitating or looking down.

"If a helicopter wouldn't get shot out of the sky, I would've hired one," I said. "Probably should have anyway. It'd be safer than skin contact with that sludge."

"I think I figured it out," Carina said. She nodded at a pale, knobby Nytundian in a threadbare business suit and creaky-looking but dry wingtips. "See how he's stepping on the middle of his foot at the apex of the logs? That's the trick. You'd think you would need to step on the ball of your foot, but…" She shook her head. "No, the flat of your foot is what keeps it from rolling."

"Yeah?" I said. "And what keeps it from sinking?"

"Speed." She waited for a rowdy group of tourists to finish fiddlefucking around and get to the other side, then she approached the bridge.

"You're up to date on all your immunos, right?"
I said.

She ignored me and started across.

That log bridge was my first real indication of what Carina was capable of physically. I mean, I'd seen enough of her fight with the bruisers at that Argamerian bar to know that she could handle herself, but this was altogether different. The only way to describe it was that she flitted across the bridge, kind of like a dragonfly or paperina. It was almost like she didn't touch down all the way in any one spot until she made it to the other side.

Her shoes were almost completely dry.

She had assessed the bridge's properties, analyzed the attempts on it by other people, and then made a successful crossing. Sir Carina Xiao, the Bloodslinger, wasn't just muscle and blunt-force trauma. She was finesse and precision. She'd seen the knot, and she'd untied the knot.

"Are you coming or waiting for the chopper?" she called back at me.

I waved her off and stepped out onto the bridge.

Moving fast didn't seem to do me much good. By about the third step, my sneakers were full of radiation poisoning and liquid chlamydia.

"Aw, sick!" I stepped off the bridge, then took a second to scrape something slimy and suspiciously claw-handed off of the sole of my right shoe and back into the river. "There goes their prime minister."

That knocked another surprised laugh out of Carina. Unlike the laugh on the plane, she actually let this one out without stopping herself.

"Yeah, yeah, me stepping in some gross river mutie is hilarious." I took my sneakers off and tried to squeeze a little of the water out of the lining. "I hope you're laughing this hard at the hospital when I'm getting my lockjaw treated."

"I don't think you would survive lockjaw, Van Zandt."

I stared at her. "Was that a joke? Are Guild knights allowed to make jokes?"

"It's generally frowned upon," she said, face straight as a plumb line. "But you're a bad influence."

☰

THE TOURIST DISTRICT IN NYTUNDI WAS flooded with pushcarts and stalls stacked high with flimsy, overpriced souvenirs and various flavors of food poisoning masquerading as local fare. Carina tried to get me to taste something that smelled like imitation coconut frying oil and looked like a cattail on a stick, if the cattail's stem had been impaled sideways by another stick and batter-dipped in diarrhea.

"Thanks, but I had the runs for breakfast," I said.

She snorted and took a bite.

We started walking north toward the hotel and *sarai* district. My stomach growled.

"I can't believe you're not dead yet, eating shit like that," I said.

"Some people don't grow up with the luxury of being picky."

"Iron stomach," I said, shooting her with a finger gun.

She nodded.

"Well, it'll also go straight to your ass," I said.

Carina shrugged. "I'll run a couple extra miles tonight."

"Yeah, but what are you going to do about that topographical map on the side of your face?"

For a second, her jaw tightened. Then she relaxed and went back to eating as if she hadn't heard me.

"Seriously," I pushed, "did some quack tell you it was too late for a plasty? Because I've heard of some real miracle workers up near the Crystal Lakes who can make an asshole look like a pair of lips. If you ever want to get a living, breathing, non-scar-fetishist interested in you—without double-bagging your head or giving the guy alchopoisoning—you should think seriously about facial reconstruction."

She finished chewing a bite of the cattail, swallowed, then said, "Do you think I haven't noticed that every time you get defensive, you try to insult my scars?"

"What do you want me to do? They're hard to look at, and I'm not a liar by nature."

"I don't need plastic surgery, Van Zandt. I don't want it."

"Yeah, but what about taking pity on the rest of us? We're the ones who have to look at you."

She stopped walking and turned to face me, pointing at the sinewy mass of pink tissue that was her left cheek, and for a second, I thought maybe she was going to let me touch it.

"This is proof that I survived what other people couldn't," Carina said. "This is a reminder of an enemy who couldn't beat me, of suffering that made me stronger. I'm not ashamed of my scars. I won't cover them up or try to get rid of them. I'll wear them with pride until the day I die."

If Carina would've left it at that, I think maybe I could've just been fascinated by her. I didn't even realize that there were people out there who thought that way, not really, just poor people who had to lie to themselves about their looks so they didn't stick their head in an exitbag and cure their ugliness problem once and for all. None of the women my father had brought home ever showed that kind of backbone. Not for long, anyway.

But Carina couldn't leave it at that. She had to go and add, "Maybe you should take some time to figure out why you're so insecure."

NEEDLESS TO SAY, I WAS IN A SHITTY MOOD BY the time we made it to the hotel and *sarai* district. Normally, that place would be enough to make anybody feel ten feet tall and hung like a blue whale, what with all the prostitutes of both sexes fawning over your godlike body, virile features, and obvious sexual prowess. But it was all a fucking act. They were pawing foreign businessmen twice my weight and half my height, minus my roguish charm. It was disgusting the way the bimbos were throwing themselves at those fat slobs.

Well, maybe they weren't bimbos. They were working their angle, using what genetics gave them to put food on the table, and they were obviously good at what they did. It was the fat-asses who were disgusting.

47

The only way those sacks of fishshit could get laid was to creep off to a foreign country on a business trip and hit up a hooker half their age.

I checked my wristpiece to make sure we were headed in the right direction, took a side street past a casino whose gaming had spilled out onto the walkway, then made a left. The Palisades was dead ahead—the tallest building in all of Nytundi at sixty-three floors, according to a little plaque in the cornerstone.

A one-plus who looked like his wiring was only second- or third-hand was working the door. He glanced our way, his right eye's optics zooming in and checking us against any threats he'd been programmed to bounce on out. Nothing about us seemed to set off any alarms in his cyborgnetics. He went back to watching the street.

Carina followed me through the Palisade's revolving front door into a lobby of sepia-toned marble. Not only was the Palisades the tallest building in this mudhole, it was also the only hotel on the island with legitimate Sarlean stars. Just three, but you had to take what you could get. Like the one-plus at the door, the whores at the Palisades were a lot higher class— expensive clothes, toned-down makeup, soft-looking hair, and velvety complexions—obviously more exclusive than the ones working the street.

A pale, sun-haired beauty with smoky eyeshadow crept up to us and struck a not-quite-natural pose that stuck out her little boobs like freshly-scratched chigger bites.

"Hey, hello," she purred, her accent bending the Anglish adorably. "I have not seen you before, lover. I would remember you. I never forget such a strong, beautiful woman."

And she was cozying up to Carina. Of course. Fuck this country.

Before Carina could answer, the whore leaned in close to me and ran her hand down my arm. "I never forget such a handsome man, too, but I am exclusive this night for another, and he gets so jealous if I even talk to other men." She pouted. "You will come back tomorrow for me?"

Finally, I caught on. This was all part of her act, filling up her screw card so she wouldn't go a night without a paying trick.

I patted my pockets. "Sorry, sister. I left my wallet in my other time zone."

She huffed and stuck her hip out at me by way of dismissal. Her fingers snaked up Carina's arm, light against dark. "He doesn't mind other women on my skin. Their smell is so intoxicating, I think he likes it even."

"Thanks for the offer," Carina said. "But I'm engaged." At the whore's confused look, Carina tried to find another way to say it that might translate. "I'm going to get married. I'm faithful to one man. Exclusive to him."

"She's not interested," I said in a language the whore would understand. *"Go hustle somebody else."*

The little whore shot me a sneer, then prowled off.

"This is where our contact wanted to meet?" Carina asked me, eyebrow cocked.

I shook my head. "I picked this place. The whores are just the gravy on top. Come on."

I led the way across the lobby to the Palisades's obligatorily dark bar.

We slid into a plush, blood-red booth and scanned the place. Plenty of hookers and clientele of the slightly richer variety. From what I could see, Carina and I were the only Emdoni foreigners, which would make it easy for our contact to spot us.

Nytundi bars existed mainly as a transacting place for high-stakes business, not all-night drinking contests, and had adapted to suit the purpose. No waitstaff circulated. No one came to take our order. The booths were tall and solid, and the tables few and far between, so no one could accidentally overhear anything they shouldn't.

People came and went, but no one seemed to be looking for a thief and a Guild knight.

"Exactly how many languages do you speak?" Carina asked after a while.

I shrugged. "However many I need to. You want a drink? These people aren't exactly known for their punctuality. We could be here a while."

"I could go for a beer," she said.

"Great, I'll take a bottled water. Imported. And make sure you tip the guy, even though he didn't do anything to deserve it, or I'll end up with something from the 700s."

Carina snorted, then headed up to the bar to put in our order. She came back with a local stout that would probably give her cancer and a bottled water imported from Soam.

"Couldn't spare the extra fiver to get an Emdoni import, huh?" I said.

"Soam's drinking water has a better starting purity than Emden's," she said. "It requires a third of the filtration processes."

"So, no?"

"So, why don't you just drink beer like a normal person?"

I felt my face pull into a sneer. "Alcohol is the drink of the weak. It makes you lazy and sloppy."

She shrugged and took a drink from her squat little beer. "Doesn't me. It also keeps longer than water and has less potential for contamination."

"And your Guild heritage is hunky-dory with the side effects of imbibing?"

"Everything in moderation," she said.

"Especially moderation," I finished the poet Greene's quote for her.

She nodded and pointed at me. After another sip of her beer, she asked, "Why are you so obsessed with the Guild? Is it because they prosecuted your father?"

I considered flipping the table over and leaving, but I didn't do either. For one, I was a fucking professional—unlike some asshole knights who apparently wanted to make this personal—and for two, the table was bolted to the floor.

So I laughed instead.

"I studied his files," Carina said. "I know what he was like."

Now that was funny. I pounded the tabletop and tried to stop giggling long enough to breathe. You can read books about sharks. You can watch shark infograms where they bite mammoth kraken in half and go frenzy over a single drop of blood. You can dedicate your whole life to studying sharks from the comfort of your apartment. But until you get in the water with a shark, you don't actually know what sharks are like.

Carina wasn't deterred by my laughter. "My first case working with the Taern Enforcers, there was a young woman…"

Even though I knew beyond a shadow of a doubt that she wasn't talking about Carmelita, Carmelita's face was still the one that popped into my brain. Beautiful burnt sienna skin, full lips, pearly white teeth. Sincerely kind, carob-colored eyes—the sort of earnest kindness that you only see once or twice in a lifetime.

"Let me stop you right there," I said, wiping the water from my eyes. My cheeks hurt from laughing so hard. "You got to see one of the bodies, right? A coroner showed you the wounds and ligature marks and explained how everything went down, so now you know what she went through, and working backward from that, you think you can assess what my father was like."

Carina's irises darkened to a shade like an emerald wrapped in black velvet. "This was after your father died. The copycat spree."

I nodded. I had kept close tabs on those myself. The resemblances to my father's work were a little too close for comfort. Needed to make sure the old man was really dead.

"That's when you started studying his file," I said.

She made an agreeing gesture with her beer. "The Enforcers were at a dead end. Your father was dead. Six bodies found that couldn't possibly be him, but all of which followed exactly his modus and means. The case came up in our criminal psychology class—"

"Wait, you guys take classes? Like with schoolwork and everything?"

"As many as you can stand to between actives," she said. "Depending on what you want to do with your service. At the time I was looking into urban defense and law enforcement, so when the case came up, I volunteered for an internship with the task force."

The image of Carina assessing the rolling log bridge nagged at me.

"You were the unnamed 'invaluable source' who led to the copycat's arrest," I said.

"She thought she was him," Carina said, her voice almost soft.

"Yeah, I remember. Harley. She's the one who messaged her mom."

Probably everyone who'd been alive at that time remembered the message. The eerie calm in her voice right up until the end when she had started to cry. The news blogs and broadcasts had played the audio over and over again, searching for any information about her abduction. Up until Harley, no clues had ever been found about my father's women. No one had even realized their disappearances were connected.

Months, then years had passed. No one ever found Harley's body. They assumed she was dead, body swallowed up by some unknown bog. They set up charities and abduction hotlines in her memory. They wouldn't have if they'd known what really happened.

From the very beginning, Harley had been different from the other women my father brought home. She had managed to get the call out, for one. She'd lived longer than any of the rest, maybe holding onto the hope that someone was going to save her because of that call. They didn't, obviously. But when Harley finally lost the will to live, she didn't die. Not the way the other women did.

"She absorbed his personality." Carina almost looked sick to her iron stomach. "She became him. That's why your father let her go, isn't it? Then she picked up where he left off."

I snorted. "Hey, if it makes you feel any better, my father straight-up told Harley that she wasn't Lorne Van Zandt, just a worthless piece of tabula rasa come to life, but you know how stubborn women are."

Carina didn't crack a smile.

I took a drink of the imported Soam water and winced. "Tastes like cheap plastic and orphan tears."

"Get your drink for yourself next time," Carina said. "As a matter of fact, the next round is on you."

But neither of our hearts was really in it. All the fun was gone from the evening in the whorehouse. Memory lane'll do that to you.

IT WAS NEARLY MIDNIGHT BY THE TIME OUR contact showed up. We had both pulled ourselves up out of the muck by then, ordered and eaten a decent meal, and finally gotten the bartender straightened out on where I wanted my bottles of water imported from, so the contact's mood problem wasn't our fault. You live under the storm clouds you drag around, as the saying goes.

He stopped in front of our booth, tilting his lousy little head to the side. "You are the Emden citizens looking for the information?"

"Yeah, and let's holler that around a little louder," I said. "Not as if we don't already stick out in this place like the plastic wrap in the condom lineup. Of course, I'd be surprised if half the country doesn't already know we're here as long as we've been sitting around waiting."

"The…" He tried to think of the word in Anglish. "The dead man robot who stands at the door…he would not let me in without a suit."

I studied the mismatched bits of synthetic cloth currently occupying the generally accepted suit stations on his person. "So you rolled a bum?"

"My woman made this." He smoothed his hand over the buttons that tracked across his scrawny potbelly. "It is my best suit."

"Is your woman blind or just tasteless?"

Carina shot me a warning glance. "If it's at all possible for you, Van Zandt, shut your mouth. Let's get the information so we can plan our next move."

"She hates your country and she wants to leave," I told our contact. "And who can blame her, amiright?"

He frowned at me, but Carina cut in before he could think of a suitably angry comeback.

"Please ignore him," she said. "He has a terrible brain disease that makes idiocy pour out of his mouth like drool. He can't even hear himself most of the time. Would you like a drink?"

This appeased the contact enough for him to take a seat. Like any good Nytundi male, he was used to women acting in subservient and placating roles, and probably rejecting his every advance. Except for maybe his poor, blind woman.

"That drink is coming out of your payment," I said. Because this guy was almost certainly also used to being bullied by those bigger and better than him, and I fit that bill in every stretch of the imagination.

"I will take a cane rum," he said. "Without bitters."

"Of course." Carina inclined her head, almost as if she were bowing, and got up to put in the order. Her voice had changed. Even her movements were different. More…submissive. I watched her go, wondering at what point in the thirty seconds since meeting this guy she had realized that was the best way to cross this rolling log bridge.

And also wondering how much of the Carina that I'd seen so far was real and how much was carefully assessed bridge-crossing.

"I am prepared for the exchange," the contact said, leaning forward with his elbows on the table. "If you are also prepared, that is."

I pulled out the wad of cash I'd brought for this occasion. You can't deal with Nytundians in digital coinage; most of them don't have the technology or the capacity to understand fiat currency in its digital form, even though their own paper money is a hilarious placeholder worth less per billion than silt on a sediment farm.

The cash lode in my fist drew the dark eyes of the little whore who'd propositioned Carina and me earlier from all the way across the bar. She scowled at me, then went back to fawning over her date, some ugly bruiser I filed under *Carina's Problems* if for some reason we had to fight our way out of this place.

"The witch you seek is most often found in Courten, Soam," the contact said. "She is a woman, but she fixes things for the people there, like—" His eyes flicked up to the bruiser at the bar, then back to me. "—certain men do here. For money, for power, for favors."

Carina was standing at the bar with the contact's cane rum in her hand, looking at me to see if she should approach. I gave her the smallest negative facial twitch. Nytundians don't like to discuss business around women, even if that woman is the reason for the business, and I don't like to be obsolete. If she wanted the name or location of the witch who could lead her to the brujahs, she was going to have to keep me alive to get it.

"And this witch knows how to reach the group of aguas brujahs I'm looking for?" I asked. "I don't want just any knitting circle of wannabe sirens. I'm looking for a specific group from Soam's Giku area invested in damaging the Guild."

"The Courten witch works for many people, including those with a…a not-favorable…" He gestured as if that would help me understand. "…a bad interest in the Guild and their mission work. She has even knowledge of a brujah who brought an important Guild knight to his destruction."

"How do you know?" I asked.

The contact raised his eyebrows as if he was about to impart a huge secret. "She spent some time here fixing something that made it out of her country alive. Conversations with faraway clients are not always secure on old-country communication devices, yeah?"

"Cool, cool." I nodded. "And who should I ask for when I get to Courten?"

"Re Suli," he whispered. Nytundians are also ass-backward paranoid about the usage of names and their power to invoke the souls of those attached.

His eyes darted around the interior of the bar and landed on Carina. She turned on an accommodating smile and sauntered over with his rum.

"Enjoy your drink." I stood up and pulled a couple bills from the wad for the rum, then tossed him the cash.

The contact grabbed the money up, stuck it in his jacket pocket without counting, then gulped down his drink. Tonight was probably going to be a celebratory one for him. He could finally afford that used tin can he'd always had his eye on.

"By the way," I said, leaning down in front of him and squeezing his bony shoulder, "If this info is trash, I'll send my fixers back for a refund, and they won't be nice about taking it." I slapped his cheek, then stood up. "And here's some friendly advice—get yourself a real suit and tell your woman to beat feet. She clearly hates your guts."

ONCE WE WERE IN THE PALISADE'S ELEVATOR, I pulled out the cash wad, unfolded it, and stuck the bills I'd taken out for show back into their place.

Carina was staring.

"What?" I said.

"What do you mean, what?" she said. "Why do you have so many bankrolls with you?"

"This is the only hard cash I brought with me." I shook my head. "I don't just walk around with unlimited untraceable paper currency, Carina. That would be insane."

"But I saw you give that to our contact," she said. "It even had the same roll clip on it."

"Oh, that! Yeah, I took it back. See?"

"You what? Took it *back*?"

I rolled the money across my knuckles, then clapped my hands and made it disappear. "Pretty cool, right? Check your pocket."

Carina pulled the wad out of her pocket and stared at it like it was some kind of abomination.

"I thought you didn't use magic," she said.

"Only cheaters use magic. That was just some sleight of hand."

At this point, Carina was showing a severe lack of amazement for my abilities. She reached over and hit the lobby button on the elevator.

"Our suites are on fifty-eight," I said.

"I'm taking it back down. Maybe I can catch him before he leaves."

"What? Why?"

"You trade money for goods and services," Carina said. "He provided us with a service. Now we pay him. That's how it works."

I snorted. "That's how it works if you're a sucker."

The elevator stopped at our floor, but Carina wouldn't get out.

"You're serious?" I threw my hands up. "I can't believe this! We don't even know if the info he gave us is good or not. He's probably screwing us over worse, playing both sides of this game, selling info about us to the aguas brujahs!"

She didn't say anything, just pushed the lobby button again.

I got out. "Okay, fine, go do whatever your little bleeding knight heart tells you to, like some kind of ass-kissing suckerfish. Be a part of their system. Adhere to society's mores."

The doors started to shut, but I didn't stop.

"I thought you Guild types weren't supposed to get caught up in this world. You're supposed to be above the things of it."

"We're supposed to be above reproach," Carina said, giving me a look so sickeningly sincere that my skin crawled. "We pay our debts. Always."

What I could see of her dark face narrowed to a couple inches as the gap between the panels closed.

"That's a nice white dress you've got on, acid-face!" I yelled at the last little sliver of her. "Let me know how clean it stays when you're slaying brujahs hand over fist!"

I kicked the burnished gold of the elevator doors, then headed for my suite.

≡

I DON'T HAVE NIGHTMARES. DREAMS, EITHER. I've read about people in the old legends and even in the newer books who claim to have dreams, but I don't know how much of that is reality and how much is a plot device cooked up by overactive imaginations. I lie down at night and after a while there's nothing and then I wake up, fully rested. So when I can't sleep, it pisses me off. I need my four hours.

In spite of the scalding shower, soft mattress, heavy comforter, and perfectly chilled room, my brain would not shut off. It was a little like when I was a kid and I couldn't stop moving, like there was too much energy built up and no way to expend it all, but this time with thoughts.

How dare she—how fucking dare she—and after all that bullshit about my father—dredging up Harley—and she wasn't even impressed with the pickpocketing—that was a kick in the danglers right there—she didn't even fucking care that I was so good at what I did that I'd made her *and* that siltbrained moron believe that he was going home with a bankroll—fucking ridiculous—absolutely fucking ridiculous—fucking white-dressed little crucify-me martyr.

"We pay our debts," I sneered. I got up and went to the minifridge built into the wall. All the sugar cane sticks, nuts, and chocolates were gone—I had wanted a snack earlier and finished them off—so I flipped through the directory on the little window desk to see what the Palisades had by way of room service.

Some kind of lamb and rice dish and a few dessert items I'd never heard of before. One mentioned chocolate and caramel.

I ordered one of the desserts and charged it to the incidentals account Carina had set up. It was pretty great, so I ordered another. By the time I was most of the way through the third, my stomach was starting to ache from all the sweet, so I ordered up some lamb and rice to balance it out. The salt and the savory of that helped soaked up some of the richness from the chocolate and caramel.

When the dishes were empty, I piled them on top of each other. It looked like a lot when you put them all together like that. Four separate trays. I grabbed the stack of flatware and opened the door to the hall, thinking maybe I should see if the Palisades had a gym onsite.

I heard someone in the hallway before my eyes could focus. I stopped the trays' forward momentum and shoved them behind my room door before sticking my head out.

Carina. She was at the far end of the hallway, leaning with one side of her face pressed against the window as if she were trying to listen to the night outside. She glanced my way, gave me an acknowledging half-smile, then went back to listening.

It took a second for me to figure out why she might be smearing her acid scars all over the hall window of the fifty-eighth floor, but it finally registered. She was checking her messages. Out of curiosity, I looked down at my wristpiece. The reception here was almost nonexistent.

I tossed my dishes onto the window desk in my room, grabbed the suite's old-fashioned key card, and stuck it in the pocket of my pajama pants. The door wheezed and clicked shut behind me as I headed down the hall toward Carina.

"Think anybody on this island has even heard of the laptic grid?" I asked her.

The good corner of her mouth lifted in a wry expression. "Seems unlikely, but I don't want to try the local devices."

I thought back to our contact's huge trade secret. "That's for the best. What's the matter? Can't your wristpiece run speech-to-text from your messages?"

"Yeah." She finally gave up and stepped away from the window. "There's a lot you can't discern from text, though."

"Subtext." I shot her with a finger gun.

She mimicked the gesture, adding in a wink.

"I don't do it like that," I said.

"Sure you do."

"No, I do it like this." I winked and finger gunned her down. "So, whose subtext were you trying to discern? Somebody at the office find out you were on your way to break Guild law?"

Carina glanced down at her wristpiece, then back up at me. "Officially, I'm on mourning leave. Nobody at the Guild should miss me for another couple weeks."

"But somebody does."

She nodded reluctantly. Didn't I tell you that the really interesting people need every word pried out of them? They never volunteer anything.

So I prompted her with, "Who?"

"My fiancé."

"So he wasn't just a rejection tactic for that little hooker." I did some calculations. I'm not always great with the passage of time—sometimes things that feel like they happened when I was a kid are only a day old, sometimes things that feel brand new and immediate are long over. "You've been away for almost three days now. How is it that this guy just now noticed his future wife is missing?"

"He would've gotten back from a two-month active this morning. Well, tonight here. Morning Emden-time."

"I take it he doesn't know you're out for brujah blood?"

"It's none of his business," she said, a razor edge to her voice.

I put my hands up, palms out. "Hey, I'm not accusing anybody of anything. What gets you revenge gets me paid."

"Sorry," Carina said. She rubbed her eyes and leaned her back against the window. "I just...I wanted to hear his message."

"So you can tell if the subtext is pissed?" I guessed.

She shot me with another finger gun.

I shot her back. "You're terrible at that."

"It's not intuitive," she said.

"Stop trying to pull the trigger." I held up my hand to demonstrate. "Your finger is the barrel. There is no trigger."

"How do you shoot it, then?"

"This isn't Weapons Design 101, genius. It's a fake gun."

That made her laugh. "You're crazy. You know that, right?"

"I'm not the one trying to shoot someone with a fake gun."

For some reason that set her off harder. Carina covered her mouth, but she couldn't staunch the giggling.

I grabbed her poorly rendered finger gun and pointed it at the floor. "Be careful with that thing."

That move almost gave her an aneurism. She laughed until her eyes were watering. A man in a rumpled business suit doing the walk of shame—or maybe it was the walk of pride on this floater—stared at us as he sidled past toward the elevator.

When Carina finally calmed down, she wiped her eyes and shook her head. "I haven't lost it like that in…" She took a shaking breath and let it out. "Since before the funeral, anyway. Thanks."

My blood froze in my veins, but I gave her an unconcerned shrug. The women I'd been around tended to fall under a few different categories—clients, marks, obstacles, and sperm receptacles. Carina had hired me, so technically she should go under the client category. But she wasn't acting like a client. I knew professional pleasantry, and this wasn't like any of it I'd ever experienced. And here she was whipping this out right on the heels of throwing that little snit about not paying our contact.

If I hadn't known that she'd done so much research into my father and Harley, if I hadn't seen her manipulate our contact so easily, if I hadn't seen that cold, analytical look while she stared down the rolling log bridge, I might've been able to take Carina at acid-scarred face value. As it was, though, I half expected the damn flame kigao to pop up and start warning me that the electricity was about to go out.

I kept up the easygoing grin. I would figure it out. Carina would come undone eventually. Everybody does. It's all part of the same knot.

SIX_

ANOTHER FIRST-CLASS CABIN, THIS TIME ON Flight 210 to Soam. I walked a shiny steel washer I'd found in the aisle back and forth across my knuckles and wondered how integral to the structural security of the plane it had been before it fell off.

"So this mysterious fiancé," I said. "How'd you guys meet?"

Carina shrugged without looking away from her window.

"Shrug you don't know or shrug you don't want to talk about it?" I asked.

"Don't you ever feel like sitting quietly in contemplation?"

"Almost never. Even less so when I find out that somebody is easily annoyed. Come on, we've got six more hours minimum before we get anywhere. That is, if this plane doesn't get hijacked and used to plow dirt by some Nytundi punk."

She looked at me. "That's not funny."

"Yes, it is, and you know it is." I balanced the washer on my thumbnail, flicked it into the air, then caught it. "Sir Carina Xiao, the Bloodslinger." Flick. Catch. "Named knight of the Guild." Flick. Catch. "Tell me a story, Bloodslinger. Tell me a romance." Flick. Catch. "How did your future hubby sweep you off your feet?" Flick. Catch. "Or did you do the sweeping?"

"Will you stop fidgeting and be quiet for a while if I do?"

Flick. Catch. "Doesn't sound like me." Flick.

Carina snatched the washer out of the air. I scrubbed my empty palm down the thigh of my jeans and stared at her expectantly. My eyes started to dry out before she finally gave in.

"Fine," she said. "You've noticed that I'm not very big for a knight?"

"I assumed your parents went for the speed augmentations rather than the strength."

The good corner of her mouth turned up. "That's a nice way to say it. But I was even scrawnier when I was a kid. My genetics took longer to kick in than most of the other children's. My mom called it blooming late. The other instructors were worried about me. They tried to pair me with the weaker kids in training. It was humiliating. So one day when our hand-to-hand instructor was about to start the lesson, I walked up to Nick Beausoleil, the biggest kid in our year—"

"And you beat the ever-loving hell out of him," I interrupted.

"Not even close," she said. "Nick was huge. If I'd stayed outside of his reach, I would've been fine. But I didn't want to win by wearing him down, I wanted to win by might, to prove I was as tough as anybody twice my size. Of course, at the time, I didn't realize that Nick wanted to prove to the world that he was every bit as tough as his seven older siblings. I woke up against the far wall with a knot the size of an egg growing on my temple."

For a few seconds she basked in the memory. Then she continued, "So I get up, shake the blood off, and go after Nick again. I don't remember much about that round besides picking myself up off the floor when it was over. People told me there was a third round, too. To hear Nick tell it, you would think I'd been possessed. He claims he was struggling just to defend himself. We were both in the Knights Hospitaller's wing when I woke up."

"So you did kick his ass," I said triumphantly.

"Still no," Carina said. "Nick was there because he was afraid he'd killed me. He wanted to make sure I woke up."

"That points to a serious lack of control," I said.

"We were six."

"People don't change, they just get taller." I mulled the story over, wishing I had that washer back to roll along my knuckles while I thought. "So, if I'm understanding you correctly, you're saying that what you want in a man is someone who can kick your ass?"

"More like someone who respects me enough as a peer to kick it when it needs kicking. But also someone who cares whether or not I'm okay when the kicking is over."

"All right. That's total nonsense, but okay. Time for the most important question: On a scale of one to Jubal Van Zandt, how hot is he? You can be honest, I won't tell him."

Carina pulled one of those long silences.

"I don't know how to answer something like that," she finally said. "So much of how I perceive Nick is based on the kind of person he is and how it makes me feel to be with him. When I look at him, I think he's gorgeous."

I nodded. "So about a six, then. Not bad, Bloodslinger, not bad at all."

THE ARRIVAL IN SOAM WENT A LOT LESS smoothly than the one in the war-torn turd of an island nation. Whereas Nytundi was desperate for foreign tourism dollars however they could get them, Soam was fine with everybody else on the Revived Earth fucking off and leaving them alone.

The Entering Soam/*Inendas Soam* line was not moving.

At all.

"I need to pee," I said, looking over my shoulder in the direction of the bathrooms.

"You've already been six times," Carina said. "Can you seriously not stand still for a few seconds?"

"It's been an hour if it's been a minute." I stared down a local guard who was patrolling the line of inbound travelers with an automatic rifle. He stopped long enough to mumble something into his collar comm, then started walking again. "Also, I'm hungry."

"Feels like I'm on a field trip with a five-year-old page." She dug into her pocket and came out with the washer I'd been flipping on the flight. "If I give you this back, will you shut up?"

"Probably not. It smells like unwashed feet in here."

"Do you ever get any repeat business?" Carina asked. "From the clients you accompany over an extended period of time, I mean. Do they ever hire you again?"

"That's a little uncalled for, don't you think?" I said. "It's okay, though. You're tired of growing old in this damn line, and you're saying things you don't mean. I forgive you. I'm magnanimous like that."

Carina rubbed her eyes with her thumb and forefinger. "No, I'm not taking a crack at you for your unhealthy levels of impatience. Not entirely, anyway. In your file—"

"The electricity is about to go out," my flame kigao said. I tried to remember if she had been floating there the whole time.

I craned my neck and tried to look around without being too obvious. "Yeah, I totally get what you're saying, Carina. You make a lot of salient points."

Carina took a breath, maybe to keep expounding on whatever stupid shit she'd gotten hung up on, but I didn't hear what she said because the kigao squeezed my shoulder with one delicate, fiery hand and told me, "The electricity is about to go out."

A pair of armed guards were approaching us from behind, flanking an older guy in a pinstriped suit. The older guy was smiling.

I don't trust any fucker who comes waltzing up behind me smiling.

"The electricity is about to go out."

"Yeah, I see them." I nodded at Smiley and the guards so Carina would follow my line of sight. "What do you want to do about those?"

Carina assessed the situation. After a second, she slowly removed her hands from her pockets so that anybody who looked would see that they were empty.

"Comply," she said to me.

I blinked. "Who now?"

"I said comply. We don't know what their intentions are."

"Are you seeing the same slippery, grinning eelfucker I am? Guy looks like he was built with ten too many teeth. Nobody who smiles like that is up to any good."

"Those are Soam SecOps flanking him," Carina said. "If I even look like I'm reaching for a weapon, they'll drop us. We need to bide our time, find out what their intentions are, and watch for an opening."

Meanwhile Smiley and his goons were closing in.

"The electricity is about to go out," the kigao said, resting one fiery hand on the back of my neck.

I laughed. "Try telling The Good Knight that."

Carina stared at me like I was crazy. She almost said something, but Smiley McEelfucker was too close to us.

"Mighty nice day, ain't it?" Smiley said, his accent stretching out the bastardized Soami Anglish with a slow and practiced ease meant to sound charming. To me it sounded like he'd swallowed a fistful of cotton balls. He didn't wait for an answer, which was too bad because I was pretty sure I could come up with a good one. "Wy L'uxe, Head of

Immigration and Security here't the airport. Hope the flight treated y'all all right, not too taxin'?"

While he spread that spiel on us, he stuck out his hand.

Carina shook without even looking to see if he was wearing a slapdeath ring. "The flight was great, thank you. Sir Carina Xiao, Knight of the Guild."

So there went any possibility of subterfuge.

"Well, now, that's wonderful to hear." Smiley Wy pumped her hand a few times, let go, then offered it to me.

"No, thanks," I said. "I never touch a—" The bony point of Carina's elbow dislodged my spleen. I choked on what was left of it.

"Please forgive my friend," Carina said. "He's simple and doesn't always realize that he's being rude."

"It's nothin'." Smiley Wy waved his hand in dismissal. "Now, y'all, I hate to be a pain in the backside, but I gotta ask both of you to come with me."

"Can you tell me why?" Carina asked. "My friend is liable to make a scene if I can't explain the situation to him."

"As y'all probably know, the concordat 'twixt our countries allows for a certain number of Guild members in Soam at any given moment, with the strictest limitations placed on career combatants. We don't like to inconvenience folks—I'm sure y'all ain't rabble-rousers or anything like that—but it is national policy to check with Registration and Immigration before we allow new Guild members entrance."

"Of course," Carina said.

Smiley Wy began to lead us away from the Entering Soam line.

"Simple?" I said.

Carina followed Smiley McEelfucker Wy without acknowledging that she'd heard me.

"Carina!"

She didn't look back.

One of the guards gestured with his rifle as if I wasn't catching the drift of this particular shit tsunami.

I rolled my eyes. "Oh, for crying out loud. Fine! Fine. I'm going. Simple."

The guards fell in behind me. A cold spot on the back of my skull screamed *Soam Welcome*—the traditional bullet to the brainstem sported by the majority of bodies recovered from the Soam jungle.

"The electricity is about to go out," the kigao said, floating along beside me with her arms hugged around her stomach.

Smiley Wy opened a door marked AUTHORIZED ACCESS ONLY in a variety of languages, then led us down a long hall. The scuff of our shoes on the industrial-grade carpet and the swish of our pant legs were the only sounds. The noise must've bothered Smiley Wy because he started talking.

"Might as well go on ahead and get the preliminaries out of the way while we're walkin'," he said. "What exactly is the nature of y'all's business in the country?"

"I've been meaning to get down here for a while now, but this is the first chance I've had," Carina said. "I've heard the scenery here is beautiful."

If we hadn't been surrounded by the enemy, I probably would've pointed out how carefully Carina had stepped around outright lying this time when not thirty seconds before she'd told that grinning cottonmouth that I was simple.

Smiley Wy puffed up with national pride. "It is damn beautiful country, Sir Xiao. Damn beautiful."

But he didn't follow this up by suggesting any ecotourist destinations; he knew we weren't really there to gawk at cavern lakes, blue holes, and dark ponds.

At the end of the hall was a heavy steel door with a first-generation electronic lock, the kind with five unmarked buttons. Smiley Wy punched in the code, careful to keep his body between us and the keypad, as if not being able to see what he was doing made it so much more secure. Obviously this fishshit moron didn't realize that the lock beeped the tone of every button he pushed.

I played back the series of tones in my head, assigning them higher or lower positions based on that first beep. Once he'd entered the code, the lock beeped three times in agreement, then snicked open. Smiley Wy held the door for Carina, then me, then took the lead again, leaving his guards to bring up the rear.

Another hallway. This one was lined with steel doors, and there wasn't any carpet. The sharp smell of Xek's Amazing Cleaning Powder curled into my nostrils and down my throat. Sweat stuck my shirt to the middle of my back and my pits.

My flame kigao hugged herself tighter and started shivering. "The electricity is about to go out."

As if I hadn't noticed. You could've drowned a small dog in my shorts. To top it off, I had to pee for real now.

"Exactly how many executions do you guys carry out in the middle of the damn airport?" I asked.

Smiley Wy ignored me.

"It just seems like a separate terminal for executions is an unnecessary expenditure. The number of people you'd have to dispose of in one calendar year to recoup these kind of losses—"

"Shut it, Van Zandt," Carina whispered.

"It's not financially sound! They're going to dump the bodies in the jungle anyway. Why not just execute them there and save themselves the cleanup?"

"You really oughtn't be readin' so many horror stories, friend," Smiley said.

"Why not? Do they take away the fun of your big reveal at the end of the hallway? I know what blood smells like, brother. Dowse it in as much bleach and Xek's as you want, but that stank don't wash out, and it is all over you." I looked at Carina. "Bet you're sorry you paid that little snitch now, aren't you? By the way, that bankroll is going on your bill. As well as the cost of burning these clothes."

"What?"

"The smell!" I said. "Did you think I was just spouting nonsense? You can't launder Xek's out of clothes. The smell sets into the natural fibers."

"No, I mean the bankroll," Carina said.

I threw my hands up. "Oh, sure, it's the money that gets her attention! You're fine following some slimy Soam goon right into a shallow grave, but the money—"

"I assumed that came out of the incidentals account."

"Yeah, no. I only dip into my incidentals accounts for personal charges like room service and the naughty-spanky holochannel."

"Why would you pay an informant with your own money?" Then she realized what she was asking. "Because you weren't going to pay him."

I raised my eyebrows at her like *Duh.*

She sighed. "I'll reimburse you."

"Good," I said. "Let this be a lesson to you. Nytundian informants can't be trusted. They're always playing both sides. Case in point."

In front of us, Smiley Wy chuckled.

"Laugh it up, eelfucker," I said.

This didn't faze him. And why should it? We were still following him like happy little catfish to the fryer.

"I'm going to pay the next informant, too," Carina said.

"You would," I sneered.

Smiley Wy opened a door on our right. "After y'all."

I took a peek inside. Yep, standard concrete floor with in-room hose and drain combo. Your best defense against dried blood splatter is a good offense.

"Naw," I drawled, hoping he was bright enough to realize I was mocking him. "Y'all go on ahead."

"The electricity is about to go out." The kigao flickered across the killing floor.

In the hall, Smiley Wy grinned at the guards and switched to a more obscure Soami dialect that I couldn't remember the name of. *"Hell with it, kill her out here. They can hose down the hall. He'll tell us whatever we ask once she's out of the picture."*

"Carina, they're—"

I didn't get the rest of the warning out. Carina pushed me into the killing room. I stumbled, but didn't fall. Out of the corner of my eye, I glimpsed a pair of glass knives in the fingers of her free hand. Her hand flicked and one was gone. The guard she'd chucked it at flinched. Before he could raise his head again, Carina was on the other guard, one hand grabbing his rifle, the other planting that knife in his eye.

The guard who'd flinched raised his rifle again. Carina shoved his dead buddy at him. He backpedaled to avoid the corpse, squeezing off a wild shot.

I crouched and threw my arms over my head. In theory, I was out of the direct path of any bullets, but you can't be too careful where precious, precious gray matter is concerned.

"Drop it!" Carina yelled in the same obscure dialect Wy had used.

I looked up.

Carina and the guard were staring at each other down the barrels of twin rifles. The guard didn't drop anything.

A red stain was spreading on the outer thigh of Carina's jeans. That guard's wild shot must've winged her.

"I said drop it!" Carina repeated.

Rather than ask for pronoun clarification, which is what I would've done, the guard's eyes flicked over Carina's shoulder. I looked, too. That slimy eelfucker Wy was pulling an old-fashioned revolver out of his suit jacket. The guard started to raise his hand and rifle as if in surrender.

"Carina, Wy!" I was afraid she wouldn't get turned around before he shot her in the back, and afraid that even if she did, that other SecOps guard would shoot her the second she took her eyes off him, but she reacted before I finished yelling.

She shot the guard in the face, then dropped to a crouch and spun around. Wy's shot went over her head and *ping*ed off the door we'd come in through. Carina's shot knocked the revolver out of his hand.

"Shit!" Smiley Wy cursed in Soami. He clutched the stumps of his index and middle fingers. Blood ran down his arm, into his suit, soaking the elbow like a patch.

I stood up and pulled my fingers out of my ears.

"Hearing damage is cumulative, you know," I told Carina.

"Don't move," Carina told Wy.

He didn't.

I slipped back into the hallway behind Carina, careful not to put myself between the business end of the rifle and Smiley, Bloody Wy.

"Grab his gun, Van Zandt," she said.

I looked down. It was lying on the floor in the growing pool of blood. Wy's index finger was still curled through the trigger guard.

"Nah," I said.

"It's okay," she said, misinterpreting my reticence. "All you have to do is hand it to me. Or kick it down the hall away from him."

"That sounds like a lot of steps," I said. "Probably too complicated for your simple friend. I might get confused and upset. Make a scene."

79

Carina glared at me. "Are you serious right now?"

"I'm going to level with you, Carina, my feelings are hurt. Additionally, it's not my job to hand you shit."

"Y'all really think you're just gonna walk outta here?" Spit hissed through Wy's gritted teeth as he spoke, but his grin was wider than ever. From Smiley to downright Manic-y. "That your arrival was some kinda secret? That you could keep somethin' like that quiet?"

One of the dead guards chose that moment to evacuate his bowels with a wet, rippling fart.

Smiley wasn't deterred. "We know your line, Bloodslinger. Daughter of Sir Cormac, the Raven of the Battlefield. A name held in such high regard by the Guild. Wanna know what we call him down here?"

"Shoot him and let's go," I said. "It reeks in here."

Carina didn't look away from Smiley Wy.

"Child Butcher," Wy hissed. "Cormac the Innocent-Killer. You inherited blood and death and now blood and death shall inherit you. When we heard that the Butcher finally got what he deserved, we declared it a national holi—"

Finally, Carina took my advice and pulled the trigger.

SEVEN_

A S WE RACED BACK DOWN THE HALL TOWARD THE door we'd come through, it occurred to me that I hadn't done much research into Carina's family tree before taking this job, RE: Why a group of aguas brujahs would want to kill a Guild knight. I'd been too excited about trying to get around their magical lockdown to even think about it. Pretty stupid, but kind of hard to regret since I *was* getting around their lockdown, thereby proving that I was the best thief in the history of the Revived Earth. Also because I'm not capable of feeling regret or most of the other emotions people claim to feel.

In spite of the bullet hole in her leg, Carina outpaced me and made it to the door first. Her hand left a bloody smear across the knob.

"Locked," she said.

"Automatic mech," I puffed, not really in the mood to come up with a more clever way to say *duh.* "Out of the way."

I hit each button on the keypad, listened to the tones, then waited for the reset flashes. On those first-gen electronic locks, if you type in the wrong code the first time, the lock waits fifteen seconds before flashing three times to let you know it's okay to try again. You can't just keep punching in wrong numbers all day long or it'll shut itself down.

While I waited, Carina checked the magazine in her rifle, then stuck it back in, racked the bolt, and leaned over my shoulder.

"Can you open it?" she asked.

"I'm not even going to dignify that with a response."

"Well, can you do it any faster?"

"And I'm the impatient one. Right."

"I assume," Carina ground out, "that someone either heard those shots or saw them on a security feed, and that someone will be coming to investigate, probably with plenty of ammo. Additionally—" She twisted the word as if it was supposed to be some kind of barb at me. "—I want to get out of here before I bleed to death."

"What, no hyperclotting upgrade?" Somewhere on the peripheral of my mind, I was aware that my voice had taken on that flat affect it did in times of intense stress, but the majority of my brain was recalling the tones I'd memorized earlier. I played back the code Smiley Wy had entered, assigned the tones to the buttons I'd just pushed and listened to, then I punched in the code.

The lock beeped three times in agreement, then the bolts disengaged with a snick.

I flung the door open. It rebounded off someone on the other side. That person cursed, then stumbled out of the way.

The hallway was full of SecOps.

"Oh, good." I pointed at Carina. "This psycho just shot a bunch of guys and took me hostage. I don't know what your foreign victim's rights laws are, but if possible, I'd like to press charges."

Then everyone was shooting again. I dropped and hugged the floor like a long-lost love.

"Stay down," Carina yelled at me.

"Ha!" I yelled back.

I assumed she was rolling her eyes at me, but I didn't lift my head to look. I am a huge fan of my life and not a fan at all of sticking my head into the path of things that have the potential to end my life.

The floor and I had plenty of time to consummate our reunion, realize how much we'd grown apart over the years, agree that this had been fun but it would never work between us, and say a bittersweet farewell before the shooting finally tapered off.

Carina grabbed me by my hoodie's collar and dragged me backward into the hallway. A second later, the door slammed shut and I heard the lock reengage.

"All right, I admit that going back through the main terminal was a bad idea," Carina said. Oddly enough, her voice was eerily flat, too. "But I really wanted that knuckgun back. My mom got it for me. Damn it. Okay." She looked at me. "What are the odds that you can get us out of here?"

I smiled. "Sister, getting out of places without being killed or captured is my job. And for only a slight pay increase, I will get you your knuckgun back."

PEOPLE TEND TO THINK ABOUT SECURITY IN ONLY a couple of dimensions. They think if they lock a door, only people who can pick locks will get through. To combat this, they create a lock that's set to a numbered code. Then the only people they have to worry about are those unsavory characters with stolen or homemade electronic overrides or an e-skeleton key app.

As it happened, my override for first-gen—I checked the brand—Rufus-Ponobo locks was in my Taern loft, and at my and its fastest, it would've taken us a minimum of forty-nine seconds to get into the panel, plug in, let it run its algo, access the code, and open the door. By then, we would already have been gunned down. The success factor of the e-skeleton key was equally preparation-based. You can have the app, but if you don't have the time to download the lock brand you're looking for—in our case, Rufus-Ponobo— then it's worthless.

And so the security systems designers for the Soam International Airport were pretty sure they had anyone with ignoble intentions by the balls.

"Shoot the panels," I told Carina, pointing down the hall at the doorways. "All of them."

"The lock panels?"

"Tampering with the panel or the mechanism freezes first-gen locks in the engaged position. Should buy us some time—at least until they bring an override in from security to reset them." I jogged down the hallway to the bodies Carina had left strewn all about.

"If I damage all of the panels, it'll cut off all our potential exits," Carina called after me.

I snorted. "Yeah, all of our lateral ones."

Satisfied that I might actually know what I was doing, Carina took a step back from the door and splintered the electronic panel with the butt of her rifle. Then she moved on to the next door and the next, leaving a trail of cracked plastic and dented metal behind her.

Back at the body pile, I found what I was looking for—the other rifle. I held it by the stock and stepped on the chest of the guard I'd taken it from. Trapped gasses moaned out of his dead throat. His flesh tried to wobble and slip out from under my sneakers, but I didn't fall. I reached up and poked the muzzle of the rifle at the corner of a pocked ceiling tile. It lifted a good foot and a half, then whumped back into place.

You'd think people would get smart enough to stop adding dropped ceilings to every building they renovated. Sure, it saved you a boatload in heating and cooling and air filtration costs, but was that really worth invalidating your security systems?

Carina was more than halfway down the hall now. I didn't want to wait around, so I started smashing code panels, too. We covered the rest of the hall, then met back up at the end closest to the terminal, where the SecOps were probably already bringing in some techie with an override.

"What now?" Carina asked.

I poked the rifle up at the ceiling again, shoving the tile above the door up and to the side, leaving a gaping hole. Dust and tile crumblies filtered down.

"Here." I handed Carina the rifle. "All yours. Now give me a boost."

"Just a sec." She ejected the magazine, pulled the bolt and took that bullet out, stuck them both in her pockets, then leaned the extraneous rifle against the wall. "Okay."

She set her feet a little wider than shoulder-width apart, leaned her back against the door, and settled into a half-standing, half-sitting position. Then she made a wheeling hand motion at me like *Let's go*.

I grabbed her shoulder and stepped onto her undamaged thigh. I put a little bit of weight on it. When she didn't flinch, I bounced once on the ball of my floor-foot, then shoved off, putting all of my weight on her leg. She grabbed my calf with both hands to stabilize me.

"Here's a knight who didn't skip leg day," I said.

"Wall-sits are the most important part of a knight's training regimen," she said. "Got to be prepared in case you show up late to chapel and all the pews are full."

I pulled myself up onto the creaky ceiling supports, careful not to damage any of the tiles. It took me a second to situate myself up there, get to where I could turn around and look back down.

Carina was standing on her good leg, adjusting the rifle strap. After a second, she stretched both hands up toward me, ready to be hauled up.

I hesitated.

Carina had read my file. She knew my record. In the Entering Soam line, she had asked me outright whether or not I ever got repeat business, and my feigned affront hadn't stopped her from almost getting to the question that she really wanted to ask—the one about whether I would betray her, too. She had to have known that I wasn't joking when I told the SecOps guys I wanted to press charges against her, that if things had gone the other way and she hadn't been able to get us away from them, I would've thrown her under the barge in a heartbeat. You don't get to be the best thief in the Revived Earth by spending all your time dying or rotting in jail.

But the look she was giving me right then behind those outstretched hands was so guileless that I could almost believe she trusted me.

Either that or she was manipulating me.

Well, she had been fast enough to get us out of the immediate path of doom and smart enough to set a dead man's switch on her payment, so she knew I was at least half as invested in her survival as I was in mine. Plus we had agreed on that expensive little add-on for her knuckgun's safe return. That was probably the reason she wasn't worried about me taking off across the dropped ceiling supports toward the closest roof access or air shaft without her. It was naïve reasoning on her part, but not implausible. Honor is one of those things so ingrained in Guild knights that they usually can't see past it to reality.

I prostrated myself across the evenly spaced supports, hooked my feet under a set for extra stability, then reached down and grabbed one of Carina's upstretched arms with both hands.

"You're a lot heavier than you look," I grunted. I couldn't even get my arms to bend.

"You're a lot weaker than you look," she said.

She then proceeded to use me as a rope ladder, pulling herself hand-over-fist up my arms until she could reach both my shoulders and the supports. She opted for digging her fingernails into one of each.

"FYI, medical expenses incurred on the job get billed to the client," I said. "Hey, be careful! We don't want to break any of the tiles."

She got her boot off of the tile I'd set aside and moved to a better position. "Sorry, this is my first ceiling-climb."

"Well, get your act together." I nudged her out of the way, then took the tile and laid it back in its grooves. Darkness closed in around us. "If we scuff up the tiles, they'll realize we're up here and start shooting."

"Can you see?" Carina asked.

I couldn't, but I had seared the layout of the terminal and hall into my brain out of habit, and I could feel my way through the beams and wires easily enough, so it was basically the same thing.

"Yeah, why?" I lied. "Can you not? Doesn't the Guild do a night vision upgrade?"

"Not anymore. Tapetum lucidum cuts down on overall visual acuity. It's not worth the tradeoff."

"Huh. Learn something new every day." I started moving at an angle across the ceiling supports. "Can you follow me by sound?"

"Yeah." She listened for a second, then I heard her start moving, too.

I lowered my voice so that no one below would hear me. "Make sure you stay on the supports. Don't touch the tiles, you'll fall right through. Even if you don't, you might bump it or make a noise. We want to get out of this hallway undetected, buy ourselves some space."

We crawled until we reached a roughly rounded wall made from some kind of crete—probably con, based on the beady texture. There the space between the actual ceiling and the dropped ceiling tapered off. I consulted the terminal layout in my head. The jetway we had exited our flight and stepped into the Entering Soam line from had been to the left of the hallway Smiley Wy had taken us down. We were now facing the opposite direction, which meant we needed to go—

"Left," I said.

The bathrooms I'd been forced to use out of boredom—less than six times, though; I'm pretty sure Carina was exaggerating about that—lay in that direction between a closed variety store and an airport bar. And lying the length of a cargo carrier past those was the terminal baggage claim.

"How much time do you think it's been since you killed that eelfucker and his guards?" I asked over my shoulder.

Carina didn't answer me right away. A pale blue light winked on, then off again behind me. Her wristpiece.

"We disembarked the plane twenty-nine minutes ago," she said. "Wy approached us eight minutes ago. First engagement with the Soam SecOps about three minutes later, in the hallway. Second engagement probably forty-five seconds to a minute and a half after that."

So about five minutes since the first shots were fired and three minutes since the last shots. Odds were good that Smiley Wy or an equivalently important eelfucker hadn't had time to send a peon to confiscate our bags from the carousel yet.

The awful smell drifting up from below strongly indicated that we were crossing above the bathrooms now.

"Hey, Carina, did you ever notice how the period before marriage when somebody's got your pledge not to screw anyone else and the period of time you're shooting at an enemy are both called engagement? Weird, right?"

"I guess so."

"What if engagement was a period of time when you shot at your future spouse and if he or she didn't die, you would marry them?"

"Then that's how it would be, I guess."

"You and Nickie should consider it. Start a new trend."

"Do you talk excessively when you're nervous that you've missed our turn?"

"Nope. It's a service I provide free of charge and reason. Right here is where we're going."

We were above the airport bar. I felt around for a few seconds until I found the air purification ductwork. In the complete darkness, my eyes imagined they could see a dull shine bouncing off of the metal.

"Don't have any more of those knives on you, do you?" I asked Carina.

Instead of answering, she found my hand and set a flat glass handle in my palm. It was warm to the touch. Obviously wherever she was hiding these, they were close to or in direct contact with her skin. I wondered whether the knife smelled like her skin, and what her skin smelled like. Probably good. Women usually smelled good.

I used the warm knife blade to pry up the corner of a ceiling tile that had been cut short to accommodate the ductwork's vent. Bright white light lanced into the space, too bright and too white to be the muted tones I'd seen in the bar. This was the little kitchen that served patrons who wanted an appetizer with their booze. We were directly above a counter that looked like it thought "sterile food preparation surface" was a hilarious joke. No one was messing around in there, so obviously the only people at the bar at that hour were dedicated drinkers.

"Jubal, you gorgeous genius, you've done it again," I said.

I pried up a full tile, set it aside, then handed Carina her knife back.

"Here, put this on," I told her, shucking my hoodie and turning it inside out. The outside had been black. The inside was bright white with black stitching. I tossed the reversed hoodie to Carina, then adjusted the collar of the bright purple- and green-leafed tourist shirt I'd been wearing underneath. "You're going to have to ditch the rifle up here, too."

"Why?"

"How far do you think we're going to get packing an operator-issue rifle in the middle of a Soam airport?"

Reluctantly, she laid the rifle across the supports. The good side of her mouth frowned as she pulled on my hoodie.

"I'm getting you your knuckgun back," I reminded her. "Plus you have however many knives you've got stashed around your person. It's not like you'll be unarmed."

"I know. It's just counterintuitive."

"That's what you keep telling me," I said, lowering myself onto the counter.

I got out of the way while Carina climbed down, too. Before I followed her to the floor, I took a second to fit the tile back into place.

Feet on the floor, I looked Carina over. The white of the hoodie was so bright that it stood out in shocking contrast to her dark skin. People weren't going to be looking at her face unless there was something equally shocking up there to lock onto.

"Put the hood up and see if you can't hide that dead giveaway on your cheek," I said.

She did. "Better?"

I nodded, then looked out over the double-hung raywing doors into the bar proper.

The place was doing a bustling trade, about six or eight customers, most drinking alone, but a few in a small group by the wall that opened into the terminal. The bartender was delivering a pair of fruity-looking mixed drinks to the group.

I held one raywing open for Carina, then eased it shut behind me. It would've been great to spot somebody with a hat I could scoop up, but headwear didn't appear to be the fashion in this particular watering hole, so I just kept my pace even all the way out.

We turned onto the open floor of the terminal.

"The trick is to keep moving at a steady pace," I told Carina, gesturing my hands subtly as if we were having a conversation I cared just enough about to illustrate it. "Even if we just go back and forth. It's easier for the eye to focus on someone if they're holding still than if they're wandering."

"Doesn't look like we'll have to go back and forth," Carina said. "That's the baggage claim for our flight up there. Looks like people are still picking up."

I nodded. "See your bag yet?"

"Mmhm."

"Good." I spotted mine circling the carousel not far from hers. "Don't go straight to it." I veered off toward the opposite end of the claim and watched the offloading chute as if I was still waiting for mine to pop out.

"This is your big secret? This is what you get paid to do? Just walk into places and take something?" Carina's voice was low enough that only I could hear, but there was an unmistakable insinuation of humor to it. A bit of laughter that suggested the joke was on everybody but me.

"When the opportunity presents itself, yes." I gestured to my bag as if I hadn't been keeping track of it for the entire last revolution of the carousel. "Oh, there it is."

I grabbed my bag off the track and hooked it over my shoulder.

Carina's duffel bag rotated into view, and she picked it up. "And that's it?"

"Hey, sister, you were ready to give your knuckgun up for lost." I tapped my sternum. "I got it back. Contractual add-on fulfilled."

"Just by walking me back into the piranha's nest."

"I hate to dispel the magic and mystery for you because, believe me, I like being seen as a god on earth, but more than half of my job is *just* doing things no one else has the balls or the galls to do, and keeping a cool head while I do it."

Carina huffed a little laugh, and I allowed myself a self-satisfied smirk. As we approached the terminal's exit, which had been peppered with SecOps guards, I morphed my smile into something meant to convey how glad I was to finally be off that airplane. Something those guards were probably used to seeing from tourists.

Carina reached for her duffel's zipper.

I put my hand on her arm, squeezing so she would focus on that pressure instead of me lifting the fold of cash from her hip pocket. "Let me take care of this. You can shoot up the next place if you want to."

"I wasn't going to—"

I steered us away from the youngest-looking guard at the nearest door—too likely to want to make a name for herself—and away from a haggard-looking veteran guarding a set of doors at the center—too likely to be the leader of this operation.

A nice middle ground presented himself at the second to last set of doors.

I led with the money and my winning smile. "Our taxi's waiting in the pickup area, my good man. Grab my wife's bag for her, will you?"

The guard faltered, then his eyes settled on Carina and went wide with recognition. He opened his mouth.

With a flick of my opposite hand, I slipped out the pin I keep in my wristpiece band for emergencies.

Before the guard finished taking a breath, I stuck the pin in the base of his throat at the vocal nerve bunch.

His hands flew to his neck. His lips worked, but only a wheezing sound came out.

I shouldered the guard out of our way and slipped out the door, Carina on my tail. We headed down the line of waiting vehicles.

Carina threw a look back over her shoulder as if she were trying to get her head around what she'd just seen.

"I paralyzed his vocal cords open," I explained. "Pretty cool, right? Makes it impossible to phonate. Take that hoodie off and give it here before he gets somebody's attention and points at us."

Carina handed the hoodie over. I shoved it into my bag, then unbuttoned the tourist shirt I had on and stuck it into the bag, too. I smoothed the black t-shirt I'd worn underneath.

"This is why I dress in layers," I said, shooting her with a finger gun. She didn't seem to notice. "Probably better not take the airport transportation." Without slowing down, I scanned the directory signs for the shuttle to long-term parking. "Red line. This way."

We waited at the shuttle stop for two long minutes. Carina stared at me the whole time. I could feel it.

"Shouldn't you be watching for threats?" I asked her.

A long Carina-pause. An intake of air as if she was about to say something.

But then nothing. No response at all. She just exhaled.

I looked Carina's way. She was looking out at the people coming and going, the guards weaving in and out of the cabs and cars in the pick-ups lane, looking for two fugitives wearing a tourist shirt and a white hoodie.

The red line shuttle showed up. We got on and took a seat near the middle. Carina stayed silent.

≡

I STARTED DOWN THE ROW OF VEHICLES IN LONG Term Lot C, looking for something suitable. Not much there to choose from that wasn't a POS. People with money get dropped at the airport by their chauffeurs; they don't need to park for a month.

I picked a classic Fedra that looked like its owner had gotten about halfway through the restoration before getting bored and taking a flight to somewhere interesting. I dug around in my bag for my slip bar.

"Glad I threw this in," I said when I came up with it. "I didn't even think I'd need to steal a car on this trip. Life with me is a bundle of surprises, Bloodslinger."

"You learned it from him," she finally said.

"Learned what from whom?" I asked, even though I was pretty sure I knew.

"The vocal cord pinning. One of his—and two of her—victims had pinhole punctures at the vocal cord nerve bunch. She said he used it for victims he couldn't make come willingly."

"I didn't learn it in medical school," I agreed, slipping the bar between the window's glass and seal.

"Although I was always told it was more of a precaution." I wiggled the bar over until it hooked the door's internal locking mechanism. "That if you can't make someone do something of their own volition, then you don't deserve to have it done, period. Nice to know the old man wasn't as slick as he thought."

"Have you ever used it on anyone before?" Carina asked.

"Sure, when I needed to." I found the lever point, then jerked the slip bar. The mechanism gave and the lock popped up with a *chunk!* "Of course, I felt like a failure every time I had to. Get in."

I climbed into the driver's seat. One of the few things the owner had taken time to replace before he left Soam was the analog ignition. Instead of restoring it, he had retrofitted the car with an electronic fingerprint system, the equivalent of the first-gen locks in the airport—even manufactured by an offshoot of the Rufus-Ponobo conglomerate. I chuckled as I opened the e-skeleton key app on my wristpiece. We had all the time in the world, and the laptic grid in Soam was as omnipresent as the one in Emden.

Carina fell into the passenger seat more than sat, winced, and slammed the door behind her. Immediately, she started digging in her bag until she found a beat-up med kit. She unbuttoned her jeans and slipped them down until she could access the bullet hole in the muscle of her thigh.

She had on soft-looking bright blue underwear. Not exactly crotchless lace, but still nice. Kind of sporty.

I checked the download on my wristpiece. It edged up and over sixty percent. When I looked back, Carina was dumping a little packet of disinfectant into her wound.

"It hurts like a catfish spine," she said.

"Your leg?"

She looked up from the bullet hole. "The throat pinning."

"I believe that," I said, not caring why she was still hung up on it. "The needle goes right into a cluster of nerves. Yeeee-ouch."

"And you can't scream." She tore open a KwikStitch pack. "You can barely force the air in and out enough to hiss."

"That's kind of the point," I said.

The override finished downloading, and I stopped watching Carina work on her leg. I stuck my wristpiece's screen to the fingerprint screen and let them interact. The car roared to life, nearly idled too low, then revved back up and evened out.

I grinned. "I wish I'd been timing that. Had to have been a new record."

But Carina wasn't paying attention to me, she was wiping the excess KwikStitch from her bullet hole. Her leg didn't look too bad now that she'd stopped the bleeding. She kicked her shoes off, slipped her jeans the rest of the way down, then pulled a pair of those loose cloth pants monks wear when they do martial meditation out of her duffel bag and put them on.

"My previous record for a car from bar-out to ignition was sixty-one seconds," I said. "This one had to have been under a minute."

"Congratulations," she said, clearly not enthused.

"Just no impressing some people." I slammed my door and started rifling through the console and pulling down the visor shades. "Hey, battle doc, if you're done with that boo-boo, help me find the parking stub. This hunk of junk isn't going to do us much good if we can't get it out of the lot."

Carina found it under her seat. The security booth attendant barely looked up from the operatic he was watching when he took our ticket and scanned my wristpiece—which I had set to the incidentals account—for the amount.

We pulled out of the lot. Because the long-term parking was so far from the airport, its road was a two-way. I took the way that led away from our pursuers.

"You can transfer that extra eight thousand now," I told Carina.

She didn't touch her wristpiece. "You don't feel a little bit bad that that guard back there is going to go home tonight in awful pain and wince every time he raises his voice or turns his head for the next couple days? No remorse at all?"

I fixed her with a look, wishing I had a pair of sunshades so I could do it over the dark lenses like some kind of holostar cliché. "Sister, I don't feel remorse. I'm not capable of it."

She didn't laugh.

"What?" I said. "Would you rather I let him raise the alarm so you could go on a shooting spree in the middle of that airport?"

"I wasn't going to—"

"I would've gotten killed. I mean, it was neat when you did it in the hallway, but out in the open like that, with guards surrounding us, we'd have been dead. It's not like I killed him. You're the one who was going to shoot him, you fucking hypocrite."

"I wasn't going to shoot him!" She pulled a Guild-grade palm stunner out of her bag and held it up for me to see.

"Like that would hurt less!"

"It would hurt for a shorter period of time!"

Then I got it. I'd been too caught up in what I was doing to realize why Carina was upset. The knot unraveled a little more, and a wide rictus stretched across my face.

"And here I thought you gave a shit about that guard," I said. "You only care because the pinning is what my father and Harley used. That's what brought on this little hissy fit. You're mad that I used it the same as they did."

Carina raised her eyebrows like *Duh.*

The pretending to be friends, the almost-flirting, the whole job—hell, she'd probably chosen me out of the Guild files because I was Lorne Van Zandt's son, not because I was the best damn thief in the history of the Revived Earth.

I cackled. "Your dad literally murdered children in the Soam Massacres and you're mad at my dad? That is too fucking beautiful."

"My dad defended himself," Carina snarled, her voice low and cold. "Soam used child soldiers so full of drenum that they couldn't feel—"

"Oh, sure, hide behind that war-is-hell fishshit. Whatever helps you sleep at night, *Bloodslinger.*" My foot laid down the accelerator. "Say, I bet that's an interesting story, how you got your name. Let's hear that sometime."

"Lorne Van Zandt was a recreational murderer. He—"

"But you just do it for the Guild," I said. "And oh, yeah, also whenever you feel like taking revenge and somebody gets in your way. I mean, shit, sister, there's so damned much blood on your hands that Xek's could subsist on your business alone!"

Carina raised her voice, trying to yell over me. "He tortured women to death for his enjoyment!"

"And because of one instance of throat pinning, you think I get off the same way?"

"Do you?"

"I thought we were tighter than that, Carina." Another high-pitched giggle slipped out. "I really did."

Maybe she didn't even care about getting revenge on those brujahs who did in her dad. Maybe there were no brujahs! Maybe this whole thing was an elaborate sting operation to see if 1) I was following in my old man's bloody footsteps and 2) the Guild could bring me down. I'd been so excited about the difficulty level of this job that when the possibility of a trap popped into my head, I'd just written it off. Jubal fucking Van Zandt can walk out of any trap. And I could. But I didn't like thinking that I'd walked into one without even seeing it. Worse yet, that a Guild knight—a fucking Jesusfreak—had played me. Me!

I laughed again, another strained cackle, and tore ass down the highway in our stolen vehicle.

"Hang on," I told Carina. "We're still eight hours from Courten!"

EIGHT_

I'VE MENTIONED BEFORE THAT I DON'T KNOW whether I believe in dreams and nightmares or not. If they do exist, then they're rare enough that I've never had one, nor have I ever talked to anybody who could prove that they'd had one.

But as the afternoon closed in on sunset, Carina finally dozed off in the passenger seat, and she did not sleep easily. The expression on her face was either extreme concentration or extreme disgust. At one point, she inhaled as if she were about to say something. I looked over, expecting her to be awake, but her eyes were closed.

It was possible that she was having a dream. It was also possible that she was pretending to be asleep and pretending to dream. She didn't touch herself in any naughty places or let out any pent-up farts like someone who was really asleep might, but she also didn't react when I let one rip, so the truth of the matter was up in the air.

When she finally woke up—or decided to stop pretending to be asleep—I didn't notice. She didn't make a big show of stretching or yawning. One minute I looked over and she was just awake, staring out at the road in the greenish-peach light of the Soam sunset.

"How long to Courten?" she asked.

I did the math based on the last sign we'd passed. "Three hours. Give or take."

"Need me to drive for a while?"

My eyes had dried out, so I agreed. We pulled over and switched places.

Back on the road, Carina said, "If you need to sleep, you can put the seat back."

"Maybe after a while." But I would die before I slept while she was awake and in control of our transportation.

The sun disappeared behind the horizon, and we disappeared into the Soam rainforest. The car's headlights fought back the dark the best they could, but the road wound around blind corners and took ridiculous jags and switchbacks without warning. I was about to suggest some cautious driving, but Carina finally slowed down to a reasonable pace.

Not an adrenaddict. So that was one point in her favor.

As far as I could see them, the facts were these: Carina had hired me to get her into a village full of aguas brujahs. I had found a contact who knew of a fix-it witch in Courten. The Courten witch could confirm that these brujahs existed and that they were well known for having killed a Guild knight. Whether that Guild knight had been Carina's father couldn't be ascertained yet. I hadn't even done the research to make sure Carina's father was dead. Maybe it had all been an elaborate setup and I'd swallowed hook, line, and sinker.

No one can catch you but you, my father used to say. Lorne Van Zandt had gotten sloppy and caught himself for the Guild. Now his son needed to get his act together before he did the same thing.

I glanced over at Carina to find her staring out into the night like she had road hypnosis, then I checked my wristpiece.

"Perfect reception in the middle of the jungle," I said. "That floater, Nytundi, should take a lesson."

The good side of Carina's mouth smiled. It didn't look forced. It was the smile of someone who hadn't woken up all that long ago and either hadn't yet put up her defenses or could easily pretend that she didn't have any defenses.

"You can finally listen to your messages," I said. "Find out if Nickie-boy's pissed at you."

"I checked them at the airport," she said.

"What? When?"

"Either your fourth or fifth bathroom break."

"You did not, you big fat liar!" Then I sat up and leaned across the armrest. "Was he mad? What'd he say? What was the subtext?"

She paused, a Carina-pause, thinking, then she sighed. "He sounded mad, but he's not really. He gets hurt when I shut him out. We're supposed to be a team."

"The Bloodslinger, shut somebody out? Surely not."

That wrung a half-smile out of her.

"He said 'I thought we were past this,'" she said. "And we were. I was doing good. We were partners. But then with Dad... I forgot that the street went both ways, I guess."

"Think he'll break off the engagement?" I asked.

"No." She said it like she knew without a doubt that this Nick guy would forgive her and they would live happily ever after, pausing every now and then to pop out a kid here and fight a holy war there.

I rolled my eyes. "Jeesh, get a room."

She didn't laugh. "Why are you so interested in me and Nick?"

"I'll tell you why," I said. "Because I want to know exactly what kind of person I'm dealing with here and because I think that we need to be straight with each other from here on out."

In the light from the dashboard, her drawn brows shaded her eyes. "You think I've been lying to you about something?"

"I don't know. That's why I want to call a truce and pull all of the trotlines out of the water."

"Truce?"

"Don't try to manipulate a manipulator, Carina. I see everything that you do. Just because I don't call you out on something doesn't mean that I'm not filing it away and watching for it next time."

She whipped out another Carina-pause. This one was the granddaddy of all the pauses I'd sat through in her presence, pregnant as a waterpossum, but it was a thinking pause, so I waited.

"What you're talking about, it's just something I do sometimes," she said, shrugging one shoulder. "It's easy for me to see how people want to be treated and treat them in accordance with that in order to further a case or help them achieve their goals or anticipate their next moves or whatever. But I've never used it to manipulate you. I haven't acted like anything but

105

myself around you, Van Zandt. But I didn't tell you everything when I hired you. I didn't tell you about my father's part in the Soam Massacres because I didn't think you would be interested—"

"Mostly correct."

"—and I didn't tell you about my internship tracking down your father's copycat killer or that I've been keeping an eye on your file for the last...almost twelve years now."

My balls sucked up close as if her foot had just narrowly missed them. The breath stuck in my chest.

I grinned. "You were watching to see if I was a serial killer like my old man."

"Yes."

"You hired me hoping to catch me in the act."

"Nope, I hired you because you were the best thief in Emden and I needed to get into a place that only you were good enough to get into." She slowed the car as we cut around a particularly sharp switchback, then returned to a mostly-safe speed. "And also because I don't think you've ever killed anyone, Van Zandt. The only time I ever doubted that was tonight when you pinned that SecOps guard's throat. You were fast and efficient at it, practiced, but the assumption I made based on those observations was faulty."

I snorted. "You're damn right it was. I'm a lover, not a fighter. I mean, look at this face. Besides, I keep too busy for such a rigorous hobby."

"I'm sorry, by the way," she said. "I let my emotions affect my judgment. I blamed the past on you instead of the people it belonged to. It just brought a lot back, seeing you do that to the guard."

I waited.

When she didn't go on, I said, "Now would be the appropriate time to expound upon what you meant by 'the past.' You know, if you wanted me to take your apology seriously and believe that you've learned your lesson and grown as a person."

"I'm not sure I have," she said. "Because here I am doing it again."

"Doubting me? Shame on you."

She shook her head. "Shutting Nick out of a major event in my life. Trying to protect him from it, just like I did back then."

"I WAS NINETEEN WHEN I GOT THAT INTERNSHIP with the Enforcers," Carina said. "Twelve years ago. You would've been…seventeen or eighteen?"

"Thereabouts," I agreed. Not that being vague mattered, considering she'd been keeping close enough track of my file to know that I was currently one hundred and sixty-eight days away from celebrating my thirtieth birthday.

"The Enforcers had six missing persons, three bodies, and one check-in at a five-star hotel under an alias Lorne Van Zandt was known to use, but Lorne Van Zandt had died two years earlier."

"Talk about a conundrum," I said.

Carina gave a small conciliatory nod to that. "I was put in with the task force. Back then it wasn't like it is now, where a task force is something they say they're putting together, but they're actually just continuing regular law enforcement and investigative work. The Enforcers had resources back then. This was the first multiple murder case since your father was incarcerated. I was allowed to shadow the lead Enforcer—probably entirely because of who my parents were, but I didn't care because I'd become convinced that I could see a link the rest of the task force couldn't or wouldn't see."

Abruptly, Carina seemed to realize how into her own story she was getting. She took a mental step away from it before going on.

"We knew what the killer was looking for—her victim type, your father's type. Young, naïve social butterflies. Party girls in the eighteen to twenty-five age range."

"That was actually Harley's type," I said. "She just thought it was my father's because that was the kind of person she was when he took her." His type had been sincere and beautiful, and if they happened to party, well, it just made them that much easier to acquire.

"In any case, we had narrowed it down to that, and I convinced the lead on the task force to use me as bait," Carina said.

"You handled him."

"I told you, it's not always a conscious decision. When I really want something, I can usually get it. I really wanted this killer to pay."

"Why?"

Carina-pause, this one nowhere near as long as the last. "Because when someone does something like that to another human or mutant—or even an animal— they should be held accountable. They shouldn't be allowed to just keep doing it. And someone who is capable of doing it once—of enjoying it—won't stop at just one."

The "enjoying it" qualification was a nice way to put mental distance between her old man and mine. I filed that away for later.

"So what happened?" I asked. "Harley came up to you in a bar and you just knew?"

"That was where my hunch came in. Nobody would consider that your father had had an accomplice. I'd been operating on that assumption, but when I saw her, I realized that she was incredibly close to fitting the age-modified description of the vic who'd made the phone call to her mom. Obviously, though, I didn't know for sure. Not until we were leaving through the alley and she stuck that pin in my throat."

"What'd she use?" I asked. "To pick you up."

"She asked me back to her place for drinks and made an allusion to illegal substances."

I wrinkled my nose. "That sounds like a city enforcer's report. What'd she really say?"

At least a mile of dark jungle passed us by before Carina spoke up again. "She made some small talk at first, then she told me, 'I hate places like this. We could drink for free back at my suite and we'd be able to hear ourselves think. What do you say?'"

"Absolutely artless," I said.

"I wasn't exactly making it hard for her. I could kind of…feel that she was different."

"From what?"

"Humans, mutants, domesticated pets—take your pick. It wasn't like talking to a person. It was like talking to some kind of clever reptilian predator that had taught itself to act like a person."

That stock photo the news blogs and infograms use whenever they discuss the advanced komodo virus popped into my head. "But your hunch said she was the one, so you played easy to get and pretended not to notice."

Carina nodded. "And then she got me."

"But you got her back, right? The Enforcers fell upon her just like the bullwolves the news blogs compared them to."

"Not as fast as the news blogs made it sound, though," Carina said. "I hadn't told Nick or my father about the operation, just that I was going to be working late with the task force the next week or so. The team stayed on call all week. I went out each night, skinpatch mic on my temporal bone so I could give the team directions on where to converge if the killer smashed my wristpiece. We all assumed that was the safest bet because those skinpatches are invisible. Turns out she didn't need to see it. She stopped me before I had a chance to use it."

"The ol' throat pin." It was the kind of adaptation my father would have pulled if he'd still been free when skinpatch technology was perfected. Hell, maybe he had seen the tech coming and started the adaptation ahead of time. That would explain them finding one of his women with the puncture.

"It took the team sixteen hours to find me based on the background noises they could isolate." Carina smiled. "Thank God she didn't have access to a soundproof room or I wouldn't be driving this car. It felt like it took them sixteen years to get to me, but compared to her other victims—and his—I got off easy." She shot me a smile. "A few more scars aren't anything to somebody with a face like mine."

I grinned. "You've really got a way with understatement." But I was thinking of Carmelita's huge, kind eyes staring off into nothingness while the lifeblood ran out of the hole in her head. "I bet Nickie-boy was peeee-*yissed* when they found you. Your father, too."

"Dad was relieved I survived, and proud of me for taking the initiative. Nick..." Carina shook her head. "If I'd told him beforehand, he would've wanted to be in on the sting, but he doesn't have great control over his emotions."

"Called it!" I shouted triumphantly. "On the plane, I called it. Serious lack of control. People don't change, they just get taller."

"However poorly you want to word it," Carina said, "I would've spent more time worrying about him than my job, and he would've spent more time trying to protect me than himself."

"Either he hasn't seen your trick with the throwing knives and the shooting people with their own rifles or he's too stupid to appreciate what it means."

She turned a glare the color of swamp ice at midnight on me. "Nick's not stupid. Just protective."

"Really? Because he sounds stupid."

"He's not," she snapped.

"The way you're getting all emotional and insistent about this makes me think you're used to defending him to people who think he's stupid."

Carina's grip tightened on the wheel until I could hear the leather creak.

"Look, you don't have to be embarrassed," I said. "I'm sure he's well-hung. Retards usually are."

The muscle in her good jaw started to tick. Now I was stepping on her last nerve for sure. Unfortunately, along with her rage, the Fedra was gaining momentum, and the road just kept zigging and zagging off at unpredictable angles.

"Take it easy," I said, grabbing the handle over the window. "No need to wrap us around a tree just because your boyfriend's a dummy."

Dense vegetation whooshed by on either side of us, thick enough to hide even the largest oncas and hogzillas. Carina was still accelerating. If something ran out in front of us, she would never get the Fedra stopped in time.

"Slow down!" I stood on an imaginary passenger side brake pedal. "For fuck's sake, slow down! I'll shut up about him, okay?"

"I have all of the hyperagility upgrades," she said, leather creaking under her fists again, jaw muscle tick-tick-ticking. "Sure you don't want to test them?"

A sharp turn and sudden downhill drop left my stomach behind. Bile burned in my throat.

"I'll stop calling Nick a retard to your face!" I yelled. "Are you happy, you fucking psycho?!"

She grinned and let off the accelerator. "Yes."

We dropped back to a saner pace. I unclawed my fingers from around the handle and exhaled.

Then I giggled. "You're about a few dozen fish short of a school, sister."

"And you're afraid of dying," she said, still grinning like an alligator gar.

"Wrong," I said. "I like living. It's a fun game filled with lots of exciting prizes, but I can't win if I'm dead."

"Taking into account that we're all going to die eventually, how exactly do you think you win this game?"

"By beating everyone else."

She considered this for a second, then looked as if she were about to say something else, so I cut her off at the pass.

"Hey, they executed Harley. My father got life in The Hotel. What happened with that?"

Carina's smile evaporated.

"I petitioned the Council." She looked out at the dark road like she was looking down the long hallway of time. "It was a mercy killing. If any part of the real Harley was still alive in there, watching the things her body was doing…"

"Hmm. Hmm hmm hmm." I pretended to scratch my chest idly with that washer I'd liberated from Carina's pocket earlier, really digging the edge of the metal into the skin along my collarbone. I felt a long scrape open up through the thin material of my shirt. "Now we come to the most important question. The one that brings this tale home. The one that hits the hardest."

Carina glanced at me.

"Were you hot?" I asked. "All dressed up like a party girl. Were you or were you not the torch that lights the fire in the pants of every observer? Were you the girl who sent all the innocent bystanders home every night wishing that they could lick the sweat off your velvet skin?"

After a second, the good corner of Carina's lips lifted. "I think I might have been."

Looking at the high contour of her unmarked cheekbone in the green dash light, I believed her. I scraped the washer harder.

NINE_

W E MADE IT TO COURTEN BEFORE MIDNIGHT. The place was even more rudimentary than I'd been expecting—a few big houses within the city limits, plenty of open-air multiple family homes, and maybe eight or ten businesses in all. If Re Suli, the fix-it witch, was there somewhere, she wasn't going to be hard to find.

Carina and I checked into the only hotel in town—an ecotourist stop—under names I made up before she could be honest and get us shot at again. Then we hauled our bags up to the portico overlooking the jungle and found a pair of unoccupied hammocks that were both an acceptable distance from everyone else and directly beneath a huge ceiling fan.

I kept my shirt on but lost the pants, climbed into my hammock, and carefully arranged the bloodsucker netting so I wouldn't be sucked dry before morning. "Too bad it's too hot to get some decent sleep. I know they're catering to the earth-humpers and broke backpackers, but would it kill them to spring for some AC? I feel like I should be sleeping with my ventilator on."

115

"With your delicate constitution, you probably should be," Carina said, shouldering her bag. "Going to the bathroom."

"Ten even says it's a hole in the ground with a board over it. Check for wildlife before you squat."

She waved over her shoulder without looking back.

I squeezed my eyes shut and listened to the sickening lack of air conditioning. It was almost like there was no electricity in this mudhole at all, like if I fell asleep I would wake up to pitch black and silence.

I reached for the washer, but came up empty. It was still in my pants pocket, folded away for the night inside my bag. I dug my thumbnail into my collarbone instead. Dug and listened.

It was a far cry from quiet out here in the jungle. The underbrush rustled and snapped endlessly. Something whooped five times, then went quiet. Bugs and birds and God knew what else buzzed and trilled on and on without ever stopping for breath. Underneath all of it was the roaring of a nearby river.

An electric sizzle ripped through the darkness, followed by a pained screech.

I giggled.

"What?" Carina was back. She'd added a huge white t-shirt to the loose pair of martial monk's pants.

I laced my hands across my stomach. "Something got zapped by the town's perimeter fence. Sounded like a cat."

She dropped her bag under her hammock and set to work brushing out her hair. "They have black oncas down here, don't they?"

"Plenty of other big game, too," I said. "That's why they have electric fences."

"My mom told me a story once about a black onca that trapped a mother and her kids on the roof of their hut. The father ran to the village for help, but when he got back, the onca had already eaten through the mother's ribcage and left her splayed open on the roof. They never found the children."

"Holy balls!" I sat up in my hammock and glared at her. "What kind of story is that?"

She shrugged. "Just a bedtime story."

"Your mom was sick."

The good side of Carina's mouth smiled. "She liked messing with me. Also, she had really vivid nightmares. I think she thought if she made them into bedtime stories for me, I would grow up to fear nothing."

"That's retarded," I said. I leaned back and wiggled my shoulders, trying to get comfortable again. "Some offense intended."

"None taken."

"Like a whole lot of it."

"Still not taking any."

"Just so you know, that attitude super-proves my earlier argument about your fiancé."

I caught a glimpse of a smirk on Carina's face as she bent down to stick her brush in her duffel bag.

"If I tell you you're the prettiest, will that make you feel secure enough to stop picking on people you've never met?" she asked.

I grinned. "Couldn't hurt."

Carina snorted, then climbed into her hammock and situated the netting. Before she lay back, she took a second to adjust her oversized shirt around her.

"Pajamas." I shook my head. "You're really bent on destroying the image I had of knights sleeping standing up in full combat gear, huh? Do you even keep a gun under your pillow, or is that a lie, too?"

"That would be crazy." She shifted left to right a few times to get her hammock swinging, then leaned back and put her hands behind her head. "Imagine the number of judgment-impaired shootings." I was about to open my mouth for a smart remark when she added, "No, I sleep with a grenade in my pocket."

"You do not."

She smiled, but didn't look my way. "Startle me awake and find out."

The jungle went about making its nighttime din for a while. If I didn't focus too hard, I could almost hear a white noise to it. I was on the edge of dozing off—at that point when the back of your skull feels heavy and the top feels like it's dissolving—when Carina spoke again.

"I haven't been handling you, Van Zandt. Not even when I wasn't telling you the whole truth."

I stretched my legs out straight, then let them bow back into the sling shape of the hammock. "Why not? You should have been."

A Carina-pause. Then, "I like you. You can be annoying, but you also don't bother with the stupid fishshit everyone else does."

"Maybe I'm handling you," I said.

She didn't say anything to that, but her hammock creaked. It took me a second to realize that meant she had shrugged.

"Shrug you don't care?"

"Shrug I don't think you are," she said.

I grinned. "That's exactly what I would tell someone if I wanted them to trust me—that I trusted them."

Another shrug. "You don't have to believe me."

"I'd say that, too. Play it off like I don't care because I'm being completely straight with you and you'll realize it all eventually."

"I just don't want anything to change," Carina said. "I don't want to wake up tomorrow and suddenly you're cordial and polite. I like our friendship the way it is now."

I worked my fingers inside the collar of my t-shirt and stared out at the jungle for a long time, scraping at my skinned collarbone, feeling the fresh scab and healthy tissue pile up under my nails in a satisfying cake, and wondering if that was what this really was, a friendship.

Nope, that was stupid. That was all of her log bridge stares and manipulation skills at work. She'd said word for word the things I would have said in her place, in a voice so nonchalant that I would be forced to accept it as genuine. And she'd said that she liked me. Unless she was twice the suicidal psycho she'd acted like in the car, there was no way that was anything but a lie.

That untied it. There was no denying that Carina was fun to poke a stick at—she poked back and took swipes at the stick now and then, even landed a couple good shots—but I needed to remember that I was messing with a predator, not a pet. She wasn't just a manipulator, she was a manipulator who carried a knuckgun and was at least smart enough to trick me into thinking for a second that she might actually be friendly. The only person who could catch me was me, but one bullet in the back of the head and I would be just as dead as Smiley Wy the Eelfucker.

I pulled my fingers out of my shirt and dug the little red wedges of built-up tissue from underneath my nails.

"You know, I always thought the offspring of a child-butchering religious fanatic would be a real asshole," I said. "But you're not half bad."

Carina didn't say anything. Her hammock didn't creak.

When I looked over, she was either asleep or pretending to be asleep. I decided to save that one for tomorrow.

TEN_

FTER AVAILING OURSELVES OF THE HOLE IN THE ground the next morning, Carina and I dressed and went downstairs for breakfast.

Because we were in the middle of the Soam jungle—and worse, at one of those ecotourism holes—breakfast was more of a prank on unsuspecting foreigners than a meal. It consisted of some citroni milk and a bowlful of fruit which, unpeeled, looked like a prickly nutsack, and peeled, tasted like imitation bread plus nutsack.

To call what the hostess claimed was "a coffee-flavored drink" insulting to fake coffee would be an insult to insults everywhere. Carina drank hers without gagging, and pretended to be grateful for it. I mentioned the lack of imported Emdoni water and suggested the hostess try upgrading to actual nutsacks next time for flavor's sake.

As we left the hotel afterward, Carina said, "You're probably the reason she wouldn't tell us anything about the witch."

"Oh, come on. You know she only makes that crap for foreigners to message home about. She's hiding a stockpile of pastries made with real flour in her room."

"That's what I like about you, Van Zandt." Carina smirked. "You're always looking for the good in people."

"You've got your iron stomach, I've got my honest nature and beautiful face. That hostess has a nutsack surplus. We've all got something."

Our first stop was a junk shop full of ancient artifacts that the owner claimed to have rescued from the local drowned city. While the owner hovered over us under the guise of helping us find anything, I picked up an old phonograph, punched a couple of the number buttons, and picked at the dried algae in the mic holes.

"It's a decent knockoff," I told the owner.

I heard Carina snicker, but by the time the junk shop owner and I looked her way, she'd put on a straight face.

"Excuse *me.*" The junk shop owner shook a nonexistent wrinkle out of her bustled skirts. "But everythang in my shop was recovered by myself or my brother from the—"

"I'm not saying they're poorly made," I said. "You did a good job adding water-damage patina, and the wear almost looks authentic, but this doesn't have anywhere near the level of brittleness a First Earth plastic would." I flicked the supple faux-plastic of the casing to emphasize my point. It made a *thud* instead of a *tock*. "No one who actually knows what they're looking at is going to be fooled."

The owner's mercilessly plucked eyebrows gathered like storm clouds. "That's how First Earth—"

"We're not here to buy," Carina interjected before the owner could finish whatever outlandish lie she was about to tell. "We're looking for a witch. Re Suli. She lives around here."

"No, cain't say's I've heard of such a woman," the junk shop owner said, smoothing her skirts again. "And if y'all don't mind my honesty—"

"Ha!"

She chose to ignore me, which is always a bad decision. "—if I had, I wouldn't be caught dead associatin'. Good folk just ain't seen with those craft types."

"I bet not," I said, my eyes raking across her carefully manicured form for weakness. They caught on her belly button, clearly visible through the sheer gauze of her dress. I blinked a couple of times, attempting to get Carina's attention so she would look at it, too, but Carina didn't notice. I focused on the junk shop owner. "So, how many kids do you have?"

The junk shop owner's eyebrows collided again. "Excuse me?"

She really got a lot of mileage and different meanings out of that phrase.

"Children. Rugrats. Tiny people," I said. "Got any?"

Carina shot me a very obvious *What the hell?* look.

More insulted skirt-smoothing. "Why, no…no, I ain't 'got any,' as you put it. I'm waitin' for the right man, thank you very much."

"Um, thanks for your time," Carina said to the junk shop owner. "We'll get out of your hair now."

"Mmhm." The owner smiled a sweetly insincere goodbye. "Y'all come back, now."

Outside on the boardwalk, I turned to Carina, ready to explain what she'd missed in there, but she opened her mouth first.

"You think she used the fix-it witch to abort an unwanted pregnancy because you saw her half-moon-shaped navel," Carina said.

I grinned. "And here I thought you weren't paying attention."

"But what you're missing is that an undelivered pregnancy doesn't turn a woman's navel down like that, only a delivered one."

"Ooh, juicy!" I leaned toward Carina. "So, what do you think happened? Child sacrifice?"

"It's not outside the realm of possibility, but not very common in incorporated jungle villages. You've heard about first-born contracts?"

"You think she got hers out of the way early. Made the contract, got her wish, then got knocked up by a random stranger, popped the kid out, gave it away, and went on living without the contract hanging over her head. You've been reading too many Soam gothics, sister."

"Maybe so." The good side of Carina's mouth lifted in a tickled smile. "You thought I didn't know why you were asking."

I shrugged. "Your outraged-slash-confused face is very convincing. Anyway, you could've been jealous that I was interested in her."

That made Carina laugh.

"I don't see what's funny about that," I said. "I'm a clearly desirable male, she was young and beautiful. It's only natural that you would feel threatened."

Carina snorted. "The day I feel threatened by a prissy lady of leisure is the day I eat my knuckgun."

The breeze blew a strand of hair into her eyes. She tucked it back behind her ear, re-exposing her screaming pink acid scars to the world.

"So, what you're saying is you do find me desirable."

"Sure, Jubal, that's exactly what I was saying."

My stomach jumped and my body tried to freeze up mid-step, but I kept pace beside Carina. Her comment had been sarcastic, but she'd called me by my first name. Up to this point, she'd only called me Van Zandt.

It had to have been intentional. Liars and manipulators don't make slips like that. We're too careful, especially around our own kind.

"You think I'm hot," I teased, studying the corner of her eye for a betraying movement. "You like me."

There was too much scar tissue on this side of her face for her lips to do more than twitch, but her voice gave the smile away. "You like yourself more than enough for everybody."

"And yet I'm not hearing a denial."

"I think you may have a bad case of selective hearing." She pointed down a muddy road toward an open market. "Let's go ask around there."

COURTEN'S MARKET WAS IN FULL SWING. Farmers, artisans, apothecaries, hunter-gatherers, and fishers from the surrounding jungle displayed their wares on brightly colored tarps. One thing I could respect about these people was their refusal to hawk their products like common carnie barkers. They knew that the residents coming to the market needed what they were selling, and they knew that their particular brand of whatever was on their tarp was the best, so they just sat back and waited for an interested party to come to them.

Normally, I like to startle information out of targets by being rude, asking them personal questions, and then making smart remarks about their stupid answers. In the car the night before, Carina had admitted to favoring the *I'm like you and we are in agreement* approach, gaining the target's trust by acting in accordance with their beliefs about themselves and the world. That had worked out well enough for us with our Nytundian contact, and I was a big enough man to admit that it had almost worked on me. But the name-calling instance outside the junk shop had left a weird feeling in my stomach, so I decided to see what Carina would do if I didn't give her anything to play the opposite of.

I went up to an elderly fisherman's tarp, cast a glance over his catches of the day, and said exactly nothing.

"Mornin'," Carina said to the fisherman.

My ears perked up at the shift in her inflection. It wasn't overwhelming enough to be misinterpreted as mocking. The change in her accent was subtle, just like her change in body language in Nytundi.

The old fisher nodded to her, chewed on his dentures, then replied, "A mighty nice'n."

"Yes, sir." Carina crouched down by the pile of fish. She was keeping the scarred side of her face averted just enough that he wouldn't get an eyeful of the mess that was her left cheek. "Looks like they were bitin' good."

"Plumb clamorin' to get on the hook," the old fisher agreed. "I was turnin' em away by the twos and threes."

Carina smiled ruefully. "Sure wish I had that problem when I fished. What do you use?"

"Crawdaddies, mostly."

"You don't have a problem with the billy gars gettin' after your bait?" she asked.

"Now'n then with a bluegill on the hook," the old man conceded. "That's why I tend toward the crawdads. Gars ain't so fond of 'em." He grinned. "Girl, ya gonna run me outta secrets. You'll be sellin' catfish here come tomorrow if I keep a-yakkin'."

Carina laughed and slapped his spindly old arm—not a real slap, just a brush of the backs of her fingers across his leathery bicep, but it got the old coot laughing with her at his own clever joke.

When the laughter died down, Carina shook her head. "The hectic market life ain't for me. I'm actually in town lookin' to visit somebody. Any chance you might know where we could find Re Suli?"

The old fisherman pulled a handkerchief from his back pocket and wiped a thin brown line of chew from the corner of his wrinkled lips before he answered. "Naw, don't reckon I know where that gal might be of a day like today." He inspected the handkerchief, then tucked it back into his pocket. "She don't keep regular office hours, as you can 'magine."

"I s'pose that's right," Carina said. She stooped and indicated a catfish. "Got a pretty decent stock of hardheads. You set bank poles or trotline?"

"Now, there ya go again, girl." The old fisher shook a gnarled finger at her. "Tryin' to steal all my secrets. Next you'll be askin' where my secret spot is!"

"Well, I would've if you hadn't caught onto me so quick." She made another good-natured brush-slap at his arm. Then she turned serious. "You don't ever sun bleach any of these hardhead skulls, do you? I'd sure like to have one, if you got any."

The old man nodded. "Figured you for one of them Yeshua lovers when I saw y'all comin'. I keep a couple about, just in case your sort turns up of a day."

He groaned to his bare feet and bent over a five-gallon bucket, popping the lid off and digging around inside. He came up holding a clean white catfish skull.

"Here we go." With one gnarled finger, he traced the bony outline of the top, showing off the shield of the First Earth Romans, then flipped it over and traced the crucifix in its belly plates. "Believe that's what you're looking for?"

Carina's eyes lit up. If she was faking that delight, she was damn good. Just looking at her, I felt like I was seeing a five-year-old version of Carina opening presents on her birthday. She'd probably been a really pretty kid.

I shuddered, then took a couple steps and fought the need to shake my arms out to use up the sudden influx of energy.

"We're not here so you can get a bunch of junk." I let irritation creep into my voice and checked my wristpiece. "This doesn't have anything to do with finding that witch. It's just wasted time."

"Honey girl, that boy a yours is gettin' downright impatient," the old man said.

"Well, he better get back to patient right quick," Carina said. "Or he might find himself sleepin' out on the porch tonight."

The old man wheezed with laughter at the thought of her cutting me off.

When he calmed down, Carina gestured with both hands like she was getting ready to throw dice. "If you shake it, does—"

The old man rattled the skull. "Yup, this one got his dice intact."

"How much do you want?"

"Aw, hell." He stretched out the word as if he was thinking about it. "Gimme four and we'll call it even."

Carina transferred the money over to his account, then took her rattling fish skull. "Thank you kindly, sir."

The old man nodded. "Y'all take care, now."

"You, too," Carina said. "And if you do come across Re Suli, could you let her know we're over't the hotel? It's mighty important."

The old fisher whipped out his handkerchief again. "Will do, honey. Will do."

As we headed down the rest of the market aisle, I told Carina, "That wasn't half bad, Bloodslinger. Y'all handled that old man purt near good, I figure."

But instead of laughing with me, Carina traced the crucifix on the underside of the skull. "My dad brought one of these home from Soam. He gave it to my mom when they got married."

"What are the odds a guy nicknamed the Child Butcher got something like that on a fishing charter?" I said.

Carina didn't take the bait. "It's the whole story of the crucifixion, written in the bones of a catfish. The shield, Christ on the cross, the sound of the soldiers casting lots for his clothes…"

"Yeah, I know the crucifix fish lore, but you're saying that like I should be surprised he only charged you four bucks. I hate to break this to you, Carina, but that slippery old mud puppy ripped you off. Hardhead is worthless. Nobody even eats them. They're disgusting."

"Exactly." She rubbed her thumb over the shield-side. "Nobody does unless they're starving, and if they're starving, then they probably can't afford fish at the market." She looked up at me, a smile breaking through that intense look. "There's no market for what he's selling, but he brought in at least twenty of them this morning."

"Maybe they use them as cut bait."

"Or maybe he uses them to spread the story of Christ."

I laughed once, hard. "You really see the world the way you want to see it, huh?"

A Carina-pause while she considered my rhetorical question. "I guess I do sometimes." She thought about it for a few more seconds, then nodded. "But sometimes I like my version better."

What do you say to someone who's delusional and knows it? There was no sore point there, nothing to poke a stick at.

I just led the way to the next tarp and asked whether they knew where we could find Courten's fix-it witch.

Ξ

THE REST OF THE MARKET FOLLOWED A SIMILAR pattern to that first old fisher. People knew of Re Suli, but couldn't or wouldn't say where one might find her *of a day like today.* Whenever I asked what they meant by that, they gave vague shrugs or gestured at what I guessed to be the general blanket of heat and humidity clinging to the air. It wasn't a complete and utter waste of time, however. I did manage to buy a replacement pin for my wristpiece band dirt cheap.

Courten was small enough that we'd made the rounds by early afternoon, so we stopped in for lunch at a bar that claimed to have authentic foreign food.

Carina stared down at the fish skull on the table. At some point in the past couple of hours, her mood had become a pensive fugue loud enough that not even the waitress asking what we wanted could penetrate it.

I looked over the menu card, then at the waitress. "What do you have that's imported from Emden and touched as little as possible by your cook?"

"You're wantin' the Emden rolls," the waitress said.

"That's what we're wanting," I agreed, handing her the menus back.

"How 'bout some of our special house-brewed coffee while you're waitin'?" she asked, leaning in as if she were tempting me. "Grown right down the valley and roasted in this very kitchen."

"God no. Give us a couple bottled waters. Emdoni, if you've got it."

She frowned. "We don't."

"Then I guess we'll suffer through some Soami orphan tears. What doesn't kill us, amiright?"

The waitress left without answering.

I kicked Carina under the table. She bolted up straight and glared at me.

"In case you were wondering, that was the waitress buzzing around your little noise-cancellation zone," I said. "I ordered you a gallon of mead and a plate of deep-fried lard sticks. Couldn't hurt to work on a body to match that mood."

"What's the matter, Van Zandt, not getting enough attention to be sure you still exist?"

"Who took the pin out of your vocal cords?"

"Look, I realize this is just another job to you," Carina said, "But the restoration of my father's honor depends on whether or not we find those brujahs. Forgive me if I've got things besides your cleverness weighing on my mind right now."

"You're forgiven," I said. "After all, you are here to get revenge on behalf of a horny asshole who wanted some foreign tail badly enough to betray you and everything you believe in. A little anger is to be expected."

Her green glare darkened. "That's not what happened. You didn't know him."

"Knowing him wouldn't change the facts, Carina. I'll get you to those brujahs. I'll stand in the splash zone and cheer you on while you chop them into bloody chunks. But I won't pretend like the guy was a saint just because he was your daddy."

She shut her eyes and squeezed the bridge of her nose. "You sound like Nick."

"So that's what the real subtext was in those messages!" I giggled. "No wonder you didn't tell him where you were going. And here I was thinking Nickie-boy was just this meathead goon who wouldn't even help his girlfriend dump a couple dozen corpses in a swamp if she needed him to."

"I'm done with this conversation." Carina stood up to leave.

I grabbed the fish skull and followed her toward the door. "Good, it was wasting time we could've been talking about me."

Our waitress stopped halfway out of the kitchen with our bottled waters. She gave us a baffled look. "Will y'all be wantin' that to go? It's still a couple minutes out."

"Nah, fuck it." I jerked my chin at Carina. "The stink of this place coupled with the weight of her own bad judgment is making her sick, so we're leaving. But, hey, at least you didn't open those waters yet."

I patted the waitress's flabby arm with the fish skull and checked her pockets for anything worth taking as I passed.

Nothing but a crumpled up candy wrapper and some lint. I growled, tossed the trash at the back of the waitress's head, then jogged outside to catch up with Carina.

"You forgot your shrine-in-a-fish." I leaned around her so I could shove the skull into her field of vision.

She grabbed it away from me and stopped in her tracks. "You don't understand."

"I don't want to!" I threw my hands up.

She tilted her head, questioning my statement.

"I mean it, Carina. I don't understand why you're mad or depressed or whatever, and I don't want to. If I did, I would ask, but I sincerely don't give a fuck as long as you snap out of it."

A heartbeat passed in stark silence. Then another.

She shook her head, trying to suppress the smile, but she couldn't.

I grinned.

"Did you see me pick that waitress's trash pocket?" I asked, wishing I'd held onto the candy wrapper so I could flourish it dramatically. "Somebody's been sneaking snacks on the job."

"I didn't see that." Carina started walking again, this time at a calmer pace. "What were you looking for? You have that incidentals account if you need cash."

"You get really hung up on the whys and what fors of life, you know that? Just take a second to appreciate how tightly those pants were stretched over that booty and how I'm so amazing that she didn't even notice me digging around in them."

"That does sound impressive," Carina said.

"Don't patronize me," I said. "I prefer flattery."

Carina started to say something else, but stopped suddenly and turned around. A dirty little fat kid wearing nothing but bib overalls pulled his hand away as if she'd burned him.

"Y'all the ones lookin' for a fixer?" he asked.

"Yeah," Carina said. "Do you know of one around here?"

He shrugged. "They's only one. Miss Re. She said I's s'posed to bring y'all out to the catfish hole if I thought you looked all right."

"Well, I know how I look," I said, then hitched my thumb at Carina, "But how do you feel about this ugly hag?"

The boy grinned, showing off a set of teeth missing all four canines.

ELEVEN_

THE CATFISH HOLE THE FAT KID LED US TO WAS A wide, lazy spot in the river, not far upstream from our hotel. A woman in cutoff shorts and a baggy crop top was lying on the bank with a fishing line tied around her big toe. Obviously, what everybody in town had meant by not knowing where she might be *of a day like today* was *on a good day for fishing.*

"Miss Re?" the kid called as we approached. "Miss Re, I brung 'em."

The witch stretched, showing off a pale, smooth tummy, then stood up and untied the line.

"Thanks, Het," she said. "I 'preciate it. Run along, now."

The kid nodded once, then took off back toward town as fast as his chunky little legs could carry him.

The witch took her time pulling in the hook and winding up the line, then stuck the whole affair in the back pocket of her cutoffs. Once that was done, she adjusted the headband reining in her frizzy red halo of hair.

"Now, what can I do for y'all?" she asked.

"You were in Nytundi a while back," Carina said. "Looking to stop something…or someone…that got out of Soam."

"So?" Re Suli slipped her fingers into the wide neck of her top and scratched her shoulder. "I don't believe the Guild's got jurisdiction in Nytundi yet."

"We're not here investigating craft-users," Carina said.

"And just to be clear," I said, "I'm not affiliated with the Guild at all."

Re Suli smiled. "Oh, I know all 'bout you, thief. You have yer daddy's watchin' eyes. I met Lorne when he was just a young thang—no older'n Het, I reckon."

"You seem to be holding up to time a mite better than him," I told her.

"Well, now." She cocked her body and put one hand on her hip while she patted the back of her wild hair with the other. The move lifted her shirt enough to show the underside of one creamy breast. "We all got our little tricks."

"A fourths leech," Carina said as if she hadn't just figured it out.

The witch frowned. "It's no fun if'n you tell."

Carina went on, her tone all business. "We're looking for some aguas brujahs you know, a coven down by Giku."

"Y'all want secrets, then," Re Suli said. "Them'll cost ya."

"Is there any reason you might want to protect this coven?" Carina asked.

"Duh," I said. "She's a witch. They're witches. It's not cyborgcromantic science."

"Those gals ain't proper witches a-tall. But y'all both know that already. This is just business, tryin' to insult my craft so's I'll spill everythang. Don't fret, I'll let it go this one time."

"So, what you're saying is you don't have a reason to protect them," Carina said.

I was so proud.

The witch smirked. "Y'all wouldn't be askin' if you thought I had any fondness for their sort. High-falutin' revenant-wranglers is all they are. Let's us dispense with all the beatin' around the bush and talk money."

"How much do you want for the location of their village?" Carina asked, raising her wristpiece to the ready.

"I meant money in the figurative sense, darlin'." Re Suli dangled her bare wrists in our faces to emphasize her lack of tech. "I take payment in the form of blood, reproductive matter, and firstborn flesh."

"All of mine are already pledged to someone," Carina said. "What else?"

The witch bobbed her head back and forth, and I had the skin-crawling feeling of having seen someone do that before. The girl at the Sharp Right Turn's club who liked *hanging out* with *nice fellows.*

"Oh, I s'pose I could take a sentiment offering, just this once." She pointed at the catfish head Carina was still packing around. "That oughta do just fine."

"This?" Carina looked down at the skull. "What are you going to do with it?"

"Somethin' black and evil. Stick it on a false god's altar upside down, paint the face a the beast onto the cruciform, use it in dark sex rites on the bleeding moon." A grin broke across the witch's youthful face and she giggled. "Naw, honey, I'm just pullin' yer leg. I don't invoke no evil shit if I can help it. I'm gonna use that there to poke fun at the old fart who sells them hardheads in the market. Me and him, we go back a few years. Friendly rivals and all."

Instead of forking over the catfish head, Carina handed it to me. "He'll keep it until you tell me the location in such a way that I can see it when I get to it."

I stared at Carina. Rip-offs didn't get much more obvious than the one she had just agreed to. Witches don't trade down for information. Worse, if Re Suli had come into contact with my father and survived, then she was more dangerous than he was. That crazy witch was going to use the catfish head to fuck shit up. Either Carina was too stupid to see it or she didn't care as long as she got those brujahs in return.

"You'll need more'n tellin'." Re Suli folded her legs and sank back down to the riverbank. "That work they done up is a seein' spell. Requires a visual aid to break through the blind. Come on down here, both of you."

I fought the urge to pitch the skull into the river, and crouched down beside them.

Re Suli jabbed her finger into the mud and drew a square, a circle with squiggly lines in it, and a wide arrangement of peaks surrounding the circle. Then she drew an X on the circle's edge.

The witch pointed to the square—"Giku."—then the peaks—"The Weepin' Mountains."—then the X on the edge of the circle with the squiggly lines—"Their bolt hole on the edge of a dark pond. Now that you seen this, when you get within spittin' distance, y'all're gonna feel it like a sodee pop right here." She tapped her forehead about an inch above her nose. "Then you'll see 'em."

"Like a soda pop?" I said.

She nodded at me. "And then you'll see 'em."

"They'll be able to see us the whole time, though, won't they?" Carina asked.

"Y'all ain't the ones under a blind. Long as you can see the dark pond, they'll be able to see you."

Carina studied the mud map for several long seconds. "And you don't mind selling these brujahs out for one measly catfish skull?"

The witch shrugged her shoulder, making the sleeve of her crop top slide down around her arm until the thin fabric of the neckline was hanging on one perky nipple. "Not if y'all had come along a week ago. But like I said, me'n the old fisher been going 'round and 'round for years. It's my turn to get a good lick in. You just so happened upon me smack dab at the right time."

☰

AFTER I HANDED OVER THE CATFISH SKULL, Carina and I started the walk back to town. The sun had nearly set while we were at the river, and the jungle was gearing up for a loud night at our backs.

"You realize that witch is going to kill your old fisherman buddy, right?" I asked.

Carina shook her head. "I think you're underestimating him."

"And I think you're kidding yourself so you won't have to feel bad when she uses him for cut bait." I swatted at a swarm of tiny bloodsuckers. "If you're actually capable of feeling guilt, then you would've been better off giving her some of your blood."

"Do you have any idea what witches can do with blood?" Carina pulled a curtain of thulu vines back so we could pass.

"No, and I don't know what they can do with one measly catfish head, either. But I do know when somebody claims that they don't invoke no evil shit if they don't have to, they probably invoke a ton of gratuitous evil shit." As I said it, it occurred to me that maybe the witch's plan for the skull didn't have anything to do with the old guy at all, maybe it had to do with a Guild knight who was already on her way to breaking one of their major laws. How do you say *The only person who can catch you is you,* but in a way that a knight would understand? "Maybe she's going to use the skull on you. Suppose she does some kind of spell to make sure you die instead of the entire coven of aguas brujahs you're after?"

"What did you want me to do?" Carina snapped, stopping to face me. "That witch was the only one who could tell us how to get through the lockdown. Who was it who told me that if I want off-the-books work, I pay off-the-books prices?"

"So you just throw caution to the wind and dive in?" I threw my hands up. "If you're going to pay someone without taking it back later, Miss Goods and Services, the very least you can do is not let them dictate the terms of the agreement."

"Next time I won't," she said. She started walking again.

I stepped over a fallen branch and followed her. "Be honest. Everything you've said up until now is a lie, and this is actually your first trip out of Taern's Guild building."

"I said I would know better next time." She didn't sound angry anymore, just resigned. She ducked under a hang of bearded moss. "I can't go back and change it now. Whatever happens, happens, and I take full responsibility for it."

"Pretty easy for somebody with a dead man's switch on her payment to say. You're not the one who'll have to go after Nick the Unfriendly Giant to get paid if you die."

The muscle in her good jaw tightened, but she didn't respond.

We turned onto Courten's muddy main road. Carina seemed genuinely upset by the whole encounter with the witch. I couldn't see a self-serving endgame in her openly admitting that she'd made a mistake. Evident flaws equal weakness.

"You're thinking you want to head out tonight?" I asked.

Carina nodded. "I had considered it."

"Consider this—we haven't eaten since the hostess at the hotel tried to serve us those nutsacks for breakfast."

"Sounds like somebody should've spent more time eating and less time complaining."

"I would rather fall anus-first into a dick patch," I said. "All's I'm saying is we get supper from somewhere in town, get a good night's rest, then leave nice and refreshed in the morning."

"Have you ever been to the Weeping Mountains?" she asked.

"Do you actually want to hear my answer to this question or are we back to focusing on you?"

"There are no roads or rivers through to the center, just a couple of foot trails. The aid groups the Guild sends into the area have to be in top condition to make it through the jungle, and even then reports show it takes a minimum of a month one way."

I tried to remember how long we'd been on this revenge mission already, but couldn't. "When we started, your official mourning leave was only for another two weeks. Then the Guild is going to miss you."

"Exactly." She checked the time on her wristpiece. "I also don't want to put my life in the hands of a local guide who might know who my father was and decide to put a tent peg through my skull while I'm sleeping."

"It's not your fault," I joked. "You just had a really bad dad."

"What was your father like, Van Zandt?"

Dark brown eyes assessing my every move—always smiling, always watching—the intentional lessons in knots, locks, and sleight of hand—the unintentional lessons like evaluating and outmaneuvering—and what did she gain by asking this now, on the heels of admitting that she wasn't perfect?

"If you're trying to get me to empathize with you, it's wasted effort. My father's dead, and you can bet I didn't avenge him. If old age and the elements of prison life could receive gift baskets, I would've sent them one for getting the job done, but I had to settle for sending one to The Hotel warden instead."

143

Carina gave that crack the wry half-smile it deserved. "You laughed before when I said I knew what he was like. I thought maybe you'd want to set me straight."

"Maybe next time," I said.

She shot me with a poorly rendered finger gun. "Meaning never."

I shot her back.

We stopped outside the hotel. Carina looked up at the sleeping porch, then back at me.

"I'm going to go see if I can't track down that old fisher from the market," she said. "Apologize and let him know to watch his back. Want to get something to eat afterward?"

"Nah, I'm too hungry to wait. I'll fend for myself."

≡

IT TOOK ME A HALF HOUR'S WORTH OF CHECKING open family homes before I found the fat little kid who'd led us to Re Suli that afternoon. He was sitting by a fire, eating greasy meat off a bone while a middle-aged woman nursed a baby in a nearby hammock.

The woman looked up at me when I stepped into the circle of firelight.

"I need to borrow Het," I told the woman.

She shook her head. "Oh, honey, Het ain't mine. He just eats here of a clear moon night."

"Okay," I said. I turned toward the kid. "Het, I need to borrow you."

The kid swiped some grease from his mouth with the back of one dirty hand, making a long smear across his cheek. "Whatcha need?"

"To talk to Miss Re," I said. I scrunched my eyebrows into the kind of overblown expression of worry even a stupid kid would pick up on. "Something I forgot earlier. It's mighty important."

"She ain't in. I might could take a message?"

I pulled the little leather wallet that held a set of analog lock tools out of my back pocket. "I got to get these to her, Het. I promised."

He stuck his tongue in the gap where his upper left canine tooth had been while he thought about it.

"Them's important," he said finally. "Them's a sentiment offerin'."

They weren't, but I wasn't going to contradict him.

"So you know what kind of trouble I'll be in if I don't get them to her," I said.

Het tossed his bone into the fire and wiped his hands on his bib overalls. "We best git goin'."

≡

RATHER THAN TAKING THE PATH DOWN TO THE river where we'd met the witch earlier, Het led me out of Courten in the opposite direction. Brambles and saw-toothed leaves snagged and jerked at my clothes as I followed him through the jungle. The little guy didn't seem to get hung up on anything, and I never saw him hold branches or vines out of the way. Bloodsuckers hovered close to him from time to time, but never landed on his bare arms or neck. Me, however, they were happy to indulge in.

The moon was up by the time we made it to a little shack tucked back in a clearing. This wasn't open-air like the family homes in town. Rusty tin walls hid the inside from anybody who might be interested in looking in. A screen door that looked like it had been salvaged from one of the Courten big houses a hundred years ago hung slantwise in the shack's rough approximation of a doorway. Moss dangled from the eaves, dripping with moisture even though it hadn't rained today.

Het took the smooth dirt path right up to the door and went inside without knocking or announcing himself.

I waited.

Het poked his head out. "I thought you was comin'."

"Did you wake Miss Re up?" I asked.

"I told you she ain't in."

"At all?"

"Not a-tall."

I stepped up to the door, felt around along the inside and top of the jamb. No immediately obvious booby traps. The majority of the interior was hidden in shadows, but a window cut high into the opposite wall let in enough moonlight to get a partial view of the dirt floor. Smooth. No central fire pit. I stepped inside. Slowly, my eyes adjusted. Gnarled wooden posts set at uneven spaces along the walls kept the rusty tin from falling in. An army of dry bones and little cloth bags the size of one of Het's chubby fists hung from the ceiling on leather cords.

Bet Carina would've thought twice about trading off her catfish head to the witch if she could've seen that.

"You can leave the offerin' over there," Het said, pointing at a corner. "Jus' sit it on the stone."

I didn't see what stone he was talking about until I got closer. It was blacker than night and swallowed by the shadows, but when viewed from the right angle, its surface shined like water. I crouched to set my lock tools on the stone, then stood up straight.

"When's Miss Re coming back?" I asked Het, scanning the room.

He shrugged. "Might be tomorrow. She says she 'preciates the offerin', though, and you come on back when it gits to be too much. She'll teach you somethin' neat."

The only bones I could see were hanging from the ceiling. Except for the stone in the corner and the dangling decorations, Re Suli kept a clean and empty shack.

"Does she teach you anything, Het?"

"Oh, sure." He flashed those canine-less teeth in a wide smile. "I learnt plenty already."

Out the window, a flash of white caught my eye.

"That's great," I said. "Well, we better get going."

"Miss Re says again, you make sure you come on back when it gits too much. She says don't forget it."

"I'll remember."

When Het turned his back on me to open the door, I swiped my lock tools and stuck them back into my pocket. I followed Het outside, then stopped.

"Het, bubba, I have to take a leak," I said, gesturing toward the side of the house. "You mind finding something to do out front here? It'll just be a sec."

He giggled a high-pitched little kid giggle, then nodded and busied himself slapping the undergrowth to either side of the footpath with a stick.

I headed around the corner toward what I'd seen out the window, checking every so often to make sure Het wasn't peeking or gearing up for some kind of little kid prank.

Over in a patch of dirt, Re Suli had set up a shrine or an altar of some sort. Two sticks tied into a cross with the catfish skull on top, looking unnaturally white in the moonbeams. A cloth bag hung from each of its spines, and another had been stuffed inside its mouth. I wasn't any student of craft, but I was willing to bet my life sentence that spell went beyond poking fun at anybody.

I checked Het one more time. He'd gotten bored with switching at the grass and was now breaking his stick into little pieces and throwing them as hard as he could at the sky directly over his head.

I pulled the catfish skull up, unhooking it from the vertical post of the cross. The coarse grit of the catfish's teeth scraped over the back of my fingers as I pulled the inner bag out. Then I untied the bags hanging from the spines and tossed all three into the woods.

Up front, Het was still pitching broken stick pieces hard enough to tear a muscle. I stuck the catfish head into my tourist shirt, clamping it against my ribs with my elbow, then went back around the shack.

"Much better," I said. "Now I'm ready to go."

TWELVE_

AFTER HET LED ME BACK TO TOWN, I SAID goodbye and headed back to the hotel. I dropped the catfish head into the board-covered shitter, then checked my wristpiece. Only a quarter past nine. Being in the middle of the jungle in a town with no streetlights made it seem like midnight.

I went upstairs to the sleeping porch, kicked out of my pants, and peeled off my shirts. Sweaty. Gross. Those were going to need some laundering when we returned to civilization.

"Hey." Carina was coming back from the shower in her pajamas.

"Hey." I turned my back on her, jerked a dry shirt out of the Clean compartment of my bag, and pulled it on. Then I shoved my nasty clothes into the Dirty compartment of my bag. "Did you find that old guy?"

"Nobody in town knows where he lives or how to find him," she said. "I left a message for him with the people who keep up the market area. They said he's bound to be back sometime this week."

I stood up and turned around. "Well, look on the bright side. Maybe the witch isn't after him at all.

Maybe she's going to use your shrine-in-a-fish to kill you."

"That I can handle," Carina said, digging her hairbrush out of her bag.

I climbed into my hammock and adjusted the bloodsucker netting. "But not some old guy you've never met before today?"

"I don't want to be the reason innocent blood gets spilled."

"You need to work on your haggling, then."

"I'm going to," she said.

"And try extra hard not to die," I said, wiggling to get comfortable and set my hammock swinging. "Dead man's switch, remember?"

"You'll get your money, Van Zandt."

I laced my fingers over my stomach. "Cormac the Child Butcher and Carina the Old Man Killer. You guys are really cleaning house."

I TRIED TO GO TO SLEEP. I DUG MY FINGERNAILS into my palms until I felt one break the skin, then I had to back off. Palms were visible.

It wasn't another racing-thought sleeplessness, but a physical energy keeping me awake this time, an overwhelming need for movement. When I was very, very little and this got into me, I used to run back and forth across my room until I dropped, exhausted. After my father found out what I was doing and told me that it was unacceptable and I wouldn't be doing it anymore, I began to lie awake, bouncing my head against the mattress or shaking until the extra energy finally used itself up.

Of course, you can't do things like that when you're traveling with someone who might look up from her wristpiece at any second and see you.

So I forced myself to hold still for two hours while Carina read. Black frustration built up inside my muscles until my whole body ached from the strain of not moving.

When she finally shut off her wristpiece and closed her eyes, I waited another twenty minutes, then got up, took a lukewarm shower, dressed, and left her asleep or pretending to be asleep in her hammock to find out what sort of nightlife Courten had.

I ended up back at the little "authentic foreign food" bar we'd almost eaten at earlier. With the sun down, the only light came from the glow of the liquor signs and the bug-lanterns hanging from every exposed beam. They lent a softer visual filter to the otherwise unappealing bodies crammed into and around the outside of the joint, in addition to zapping enough flying bloodsuckers to seem as if they'd been set to strobe.

There was a pretty little thing at the end of the bar, shooting doubles. Every time she lifted the glass to her lips, her shirt rode up, flashing a dark, tempting slice of tummy with a cute little black hole of a belly button. That excess energy twisted and popped inside my skin. I exhaled long and deep through my nose, flexing and uncurling my toes inside my shoes.

I avoided the waitresses and picked out a few of the better-looking women for warm-ups. A guy doesn't proposition another guy in Soam unless he wants to find himself on the receiving end of a lynching.

The first two girls wanted to flirt. The third wanted to fuck, but she wasn't the doubles girl, so I shook her off.

Over at the end of the bar, Doubles Girl had switched to water, probably an attempt to temper that alcopoisoning she'd been working on.

I came up on her left flank. "Kill it yet?"

She gave me a surprisingly alert look for someone who had just downed enough booze to drop a bullwolf. "Excuse me?"

"Whatever you're trying to drink away," I said, leaning my elbows on the bar and putting one sneaker on the boot rail. "Or is this just your preferred method of self-destruction?"

Dimples made deep cuts in her smooth cheeks when she smiled. "I take it any way I can get it. Ain't no fun if it don't hurt a little."

"Now you're speaking my language," I said, my voice dropping to a predatory growl she wouldn't be able to resist.

"Maybe we oughta go somewhere we can hear each other better," she suggested. "Thataway I can show you how fluent I am."

DOUBLES GIRL AND I PUT EACH OTHER THROUGH the paces on the other side of town in one of Courten's few big houses. She wasn't as athletic as she'd looked in the bar, but she was willing to do just about anything and do it at top volume, which was a nice compromise. Rebellious daddy's girl was my guess, spoiled beyond all hope of redemption if what I saw of her room was any indication. It struck me as a little weird that she took a couple wristpiece snapshots of us in unnatural positions, but she was a lot screwed up, so I filed it under Crazy Drunk Girl Stories, made a mental note to lift her wristpiece before I left, and went back to working off that extra energy.

Afterward, exhaustion hit me. I dropped like a kid who'd just spent the last couple hours sprinting back and forth across his room. Nothing quite as effective in the battle against insomnia as having someone fuck you off to sleep.

Apparently Doubles Girl agreed because she dropped onto the bed next to me and put her head on my shoulder.

I shoved her off. "Don't touch me. You're sweaty."

"AC's makin' me cold," she whined, trying to cozy up to me again. "Warm me up."

"No, you reek." I rolled onto my side so my back was facing her. "Go take a shower."

The covers jerked underneath me. I felt the mattress dip, then heard her stumble out of bed.

"Don't wanna be here so bad, why dontcha getta hell out already?" All that liquor must've been catching up.

"Because the hotel in this ass-backward mudhole doesn't have air conditioning and I want one decent night's sleep before I leave tomorrow." I punched the pillow into a tolerable shape, lay back down, and shut my eyes.

Soft footsteps crossed the floor. A light came on in the bathroom, followed by the shower. The cooling system cycled on, and cold air poured out of the house's vents.

There wasn't any holding it off anymore. Sleep dropped on top of me, and the world disappeared.

☰

SOMEONE MOVED AGAINST MY BACK, AND EVERY muscle in my body froze. I could feel my pulse pounding in my throat. But I could hear the cooling unit running. The electricity was still on.

A woman screamed.

Light slapped me in the face. I blinked as fast as possible, trying to adjust my pupils to the sudden brightness.

Doubles Girl's room. Still full of expensive objects meant to quantify an indifferent father's love for his spoiled brat. Now featuring a fully-clothed screaming woman pointing a blood-red nail at me.

"In my room, you bitch!" She grabbed a decorative pillow off of a high-backed princess chair and brandished it like a flail. "I cain't believe you! In my room!"

Behind me, Doubles Girl giggled. "You weren't usin' it."

"Daddy! Mama!" The flail princess threw the pillow at Doubles Girl and immediately began searching the vicinity for a more effective weapon. "Vai's in my room! She's got a guy in my room!"

I rolled off the bed, unhooked my pants from some sort of trophy, and grabbed my shirt off the floor. My sneaks were underneath Doubles Girl's shirt. I threw her shirt aside and stomped them on.

Doubles Girl sat up in bed without bothering to wrap the sheet around her breasts. I leaned down, cupped one, and ran my thumb over the nipple. It puckered up, cute and dark and the perfect distraction from my other hand on her wristpiece.

"Daddy!" Flail Princess screamed.

From somewhere down the hall came an answering shout and the ruckus of bare feet on Soami hardwood.

I gave Doubles Girl one more tweak and headed for the closest window.

"Message me?" she asked, grinning.

I shot her a wink and a finger gun. "Not on your life." Then I shot one Flail Princess's way. "You're going to want to wash that bedding."

I unlocked the window, threw open the sash, and climbed out. The whole apparatus slammed behind me as I took off across the porch roof.

≡

EVEN THOUGH THE SUN HAD YET TO RISE, CARINA was at the hotel breakfast table drinking hot brown liquid that didn't taste at all like coffee and eating nutsack that didn't taste at all like fruit when I showed up.

"You're up early," I said, wondering whether she'd unknowingly taken her morning dump on the catfish skull that I had stolen back from the crazy-haired Re Suli.

Carina shrugged. "I'm eager to get this showboat on the river."

155

"Good. I think I might be wanted in this latrine of a town now too, so the sooner we leave, the better."

Her eyebrow cocked.

"If it makes you feel any better, it wasn't for serial murder," I said. "All I did was get nasty with some jungle baron's attention-starved daughter all over her overachieving sister's room. I'm going to take a shower, then let's burn tires."

THIRTEEN_

GIKU WAS A MAJOR PORT CITY IN THE SOUTHERN Gulf of Soam, just east of the Weeping Mountains. The stolen Fedra got us there in about six hours. While we drove, I recapped the night in Ultra-Def for Carina. She countered by filling me in on the much less exciting topographical map studying she'd been doing. Because I knew it was grossing her out, I counter-countered by adding Sensovision to my descriptions.

"It's more rainforest," Carina said, "But there are a few points that could serve as drops if we could find a helicopter pilot willing to fly us in."

"Sure, I'll make some calls," I said. "I'm serious, though. It was gritty as sand. I half expected to find a black pearl cloistered up in th—"

"I was serious when I said I really, really didn't want to know."

"And the smell!"

"Not listening."

"But I dive back in there because at that point, I'm committed—"

The beginning of an infogram on the Weeping Mountains blared out of Carina's wristpiece. She turned it up louder, trying to drown me out.

I pulled Doubles Girl's lifted wristpiece out of my pocket, glanced away from the road long enough to open the Recent Pictures, then handed it to Carina. She took it, a confused look on her face.

A second later, she figured out what she was looking at. She threw the wristpiece at me. It bounced off my arm and landed in my lap.

I giggled, rolled the window down, and chucked the digital evidence of my and Doubles Girl's dirty deeds out.

"You're not even going to keep it?" Carina asked.

"Why? Were you wanting to borrow it later?"

"No thanks," she said. "I don't need the nightmares."

"It's okay to be curious about what a grown man and a grown woman do in the privacy of her sister's bed. It's only natural."

"What I just saw was not in any way natural," Carina said. "If they made a brain-scrubbing substance that could wash away visual memories, I would buy enough to render myself blind."

"Which reminds me, if you and Nickie-boy ever try that one out, make sure you stretch first. You do not want a leg cramp in that position."

Carina made a show of turning up the infogram on her wristpiece again. I laughed. It was shaping up to be a great day.

Ξ

BELIEVE IT OR NOT, REPUTABLE HELICOPTER pilots don't advertise themselves as "willing to drop armed passengers in the middle of the jungle," so when

I told Carina I would call around, what I actually meant was that I would spend the entire time that she was driving on my wristpiece contacting transpo people I'd used in the past and asking them for recommendations in Soam. I've screwed a lot of informants out of a lot of physical and digital bank rolls in my day, but I don't mess around when it comes to paying the people who fly, sail, or tunnel me to and from remote jobs. That's a quick way to end up marooned somewhere. As such, within the getaway drivers' community, I've actually got a sterling reputation.

I ended up with the name of a pilot who worked for a hunting resort chain in Soam, dropping and picking up large-game hunters in the jungle, and who didn't mind moonlighting on the side for people who had the currency to spare. Carina wanted to meet with him as soon as possible after getting into Giku, but he was running pickups and drop-offs all day and wouldn't be available until that evening.

We checked into the Glass House, the hotel Carina had booked for us on the drive, and took an elevator up to our rooms.

"Ah!" I inhaled the filtered, purified, and air conditioned scent of five Sarlean stars. "Smells like civilization."

The good side of Carina's mouth smirked. "Smells like rich germophobes."

"Mildew is a very real health concern, Carina." I watched the digital numbers on the glass panels slow as we came to our floor. "I can't wait to take a real shower and eat some real food."

The doors opened, but Carina hesitated as she stepped out. She looked at me. "Did you eat anything while we were in Courten?"

I leered. "Besides that baron's daughter—"

"Gross. Definitely not what I meant and you know it," Carina said. "I'm serious, did you eat any food that whole time? I saw you take one bite of citroni fruit at breakfast. We didn't stick around to eat whatever you ordered us at the bar. You said you were going to fend for yourself for supper last night."

"If I could've found something imported and vacuum-packed, I would have, but everything the locals were willing to part with in that little shitpuddle was home-fried. I tried to bribe the hostess for some goodies from her stash, but she wouldn't even admit that she had a stash."

Carina was staring at me, lips and brows forming an expression that was almost studious.

"What?" I asked.

"How do you survive?" she asked. "That's not just pickiness, that's…"

"It's called having discerning tastes."

She started walking again. "Nope, it's called having a weakness."

"I don't compromise when it comes to food, Carina. You shouldn't, either, iron stomach or not. Do you want mouth-gonorrhea? Because poorly prepared food is how you get mouth-gonorrhea."

"Those breakfast fruits weren't even peeled. They were probably the least-processed food you've ever been in contact with."

"That was different. Those tasted like nutsack."

"You would never survive in the wild."

"I wouldn't want to. I'm a creature of luxury, Carina, and I demand to be treated like one. Give me five-star cuisine or give me death."

She snorted.

My door came up first. I scanned my key and opened it, then stopped just before stepping inside.

Carina hadn't waited for me or said anything, just kept on walking down the hall to her room, two down from mine. She was scanning her key when she noticed me watching her.

"What?" she asked.

The skylights in the roof of the Glass House hotel were shining just right off the pink mass of scar tissue on her left cheek. I could see myself running my fingers across it, her eyes closing as she leaned into my touch.

"You could really use a shower, too," I told her, curling my fingers into a fist. My nails dug into my palm. "You look like shit."

She opened her mouth to say something back, but her wristpiece started ringing. She glanced down at it, then back at me.

"Tell Nickie-boy I said hi." I went into my room and shut the door before she could answer. I launched my bag at the couch. "Stupid fucker."

CARINA DIDN'T CALL MY ROOM OR MESSAGE MY wristpiece later to see if I wanted to go get something to eat with her, so I raided the snacks in the minibar and ordered some room service.

Maybe she was still talking to Nick or whoever had called. Maybe she'd fallen asleep. Maybe she was downstairs using the Glass House's gym to run off all those nutsack fruit and diarrhea-dipped cattails-on-a-stick she ate. Maybe she was waiting to see if I would message her.

I wouldn't. If she wanted this game to progress, she was going to have to make the next move.

When my locally-sourced, freshly-prepared scallops *zri* with cristgrass salad and the Glass House kitchen's take on the classic Emden roll was delivered, I sat on the bed and ate. Light and buttery with a hint of pan char. Edible perfection.

I messed with my wristpiece while I ate. If I went digging around with the Silver Platter infoserve tech upgrade I'd gotten off the digi-black market last year, I could probably link to Carina's wristpiece and find out what she was up to, check her messages, figure out why she was ignoring me.

It was tempting, definitely, but it was also a bad sign. I was having too much fun hanging around Carina. I was buying into the friendship lie again, thinking of her as the pet, not the predator.

The only person who can catch you is you.

With the savory and the greenery coating the inside of my stomach like a warm hug, it was time for something sweet. All four of the desserts on the Glass House's menu sounded good, so I ordered one of each, telling myself that I was making up for lost meals while in Courten.

While I waited for dessert to be delivered, I glanced down at the knife on the scallops and cristgrass tray, then up at my reflection in the mirrored ceiling.

My hands were grabbing at the slack in my gut. I smiled. The man in the mirror giggled at me.

Nope, cutting off chunks of myself with a serrated knife in the middle of the afternoon would never work. I didn't have any way to sufficiently sanitize the knife, there would be blood all over the place, the possibility of hitting an artery, and even if I didn't, I would have to dispose of the flesh somewhere. You couldn't just flush semisolid chunks of adipose tissue that big without clogging the toilet. Physical plant would come to unclog it, realize what it was, and freak out. A move like that would be impossible to keep secret.

Room service knocked politely, emphasizing that meditation and self-examination will always bow to the real world.

I got up and shook my head. "And can you imagine the scars?"

FOURTEEN_

I MUST'VE DOZED OFF AT SOME POINT AFTER EATING because when I woke up, the world outside the wall of windows in my room was dark and lit with blue and orange city lights. The air conditioner was running full blast over in the corner. I stretched and listened for what had woken me.

Three solid knocks, the sort that a person accustomed to being in authority probably does without even thinking about it. I rolled out of bed and checked the security screen next to the room door.

The hidden camera was set at a high angle so I could see the top of Carina's head with the least amount of fishbowl distortion. Her long hair was pulled back into a ponytail that would've looked good—younger and pretty—if not for the way it emphasized her scars. She stood in the hall with her thumbs hooked into her jeans pockets, looking down at her shoes while she waited for me to answer the door.

I smiled. In spite of the fact that I knew I should be proceeding with caution, Carina's game was working. I was excited to see her.

I stacked the plates and snack trash from earlier onto a tray, set them on the bathroom counter, then pulled the bathroom door shut. I hadn't seen Carina wear her hair like that before. This ponytail business was a first.

Three more commanding knocks.

"Coming," I yelled.

I checked myself out in the mirror over the bed. Dark circles under the eyes from the recent lack of sleep, but the eyebrow scar and perfect smile brought it all together in a way that gave the dark circles an air of mystery.

"Come on, Van Zandt, we're going to be late," Carina called.

"Give me a second to get some clothes on," I yelled back.

In the hall, she rolled her head on her neck impatiently, which is what I would have done if I knew someone was watching me on a security screen. Why the sudden hairstyle change?

I unbuttoned my tourist shirt until it flapped loose over my t-shirt and thought back to sitting in my room earlier, eating and wondering why she wasn't contacting me. Maybe she *had* been waiting for me to message her first, and since I hadn't messaged her, she'd decided to try a more visual way of attracting my attention.

"All right already," I said, opening the door. I messed with the collar on my tourist shirt, straightening it as if I'd just thrown it on. "What do you want?"

She glanced at the shirt, then up at me. "We're meeting with the pilot across town in half an hour and you weren't even dressed?"

"I took a nap. I had a big night last night. That's what you're wearing?" I turned a condescending eye on the tank top and jeans hugging her toned, athletic body. "You know this isn't a Guild shrimp boil, right?"

"Says the guy in a shirt covered with blue and orange flowers."

"The guy in *slacks* and a shirt covered with blue and orange flowers," I countered. "Most of these Giku dinner clubs will bounce anybody in jeans. It's the first thing they look for. Even if they did let you in, you'd stick out like the vag in the oysterlusk beauty contest."

"What should I wear, then?"

"Something feminine, if you own anything that fits the adjective," I said, ignoring the way that her shirt emphasized the soft curve of her breasts. "A dress would be best, but even a skirt and nice shirt would get us past the host. Think rich germophobe meets prissy lady of leisure."

She sighed and went back to her room.

≡

WITH AS LITTLE NOTICE AS I'D GIVEN HER, Carina actually did an admirable job. She stepped onto the pier of the outdoor dinner club wearing a sleeveless knee-length dress that clung to her torso and swished in interesting patterns around her hips.

"You lying bastard," she said, looking around at the patrons wearing jeans and t-shirts. The ones who weren't wearing shorts and swimming suits, anyway. "This is literally a shrimp boil."

I giggled. "I know, right?"

"You're going to regret this," she said.

"Nah." I shook my head. "That doesn't sound like me at all."

"People are staring."

"It's because you're overdressed."

She growled in her throat. "I'm going to kill you."

"Like father, like daughter."

The host appeared, and Carina turned a radiant smile on him as if she wasn't completely out of place in a casual club for fat Soam shrimp-lovers.

"Table for two?" the host asked.

"Three," Carina corrected him. "We're meeting someone. Blake Atson. Has he been seated?"

"Yep, he has. Follow me, darlin'."

The host led us to a round, bug-lantern lit table, where a man was already working on peeling a mountain of shrimp. Before he left, the host pulled out Carina's seat as if this was a much fancier restaurant.

"Atson?" Carina asked, offering her hand. The bug-lantern illuminated faded scars down her bare forearm that brought to mind the deflection of sharp objects.

Atson utilized a napkin before shaking. "That'd be me. Guessing by your accent that you're not from around here, stranger."

"Guessing by your accent that you're from the mountain bayous up in Emden," Carina said, mimicking his accent playfully.

"Originally, yeah," he said, cocking his head at Carina in surprise.

"It's not that impressive a guess on my part," she said, lowering her chin with a self-deprecating smile. "My fiancé's from up that way originally, too. I hear 'stranger' a lot."

They laughed together at what I assumed was a regional inside joke, and my internal Fuck This Guy O-Meter redlined.

I smiled as if I thought being outside the inner circle jerk was funny. "Well, now that you two know each other's life stories, should we talk business?"

"I take it this *isn't* your fiancé?" Atson said.

Carina chuckled. "This is my business partner. He's not trying to be rude, but he stays pretty focused on the job."

"No, no, I understand," Atson said, offering his hand to me. "Without the blinders, the workhorse gets distracted. I can respect that attitude."

"John Dillinger," I said, giving his hand a businesslike shake and his face a businesslike frown.

"Pleased to meet you." Atson didn't register a flicker of recognition at the name. This is why you study First Earth lore—so you'll know when someone gives you a blatantly obvious alias.

The waiter came around and took our orders. An aperitif for Carina, bottled water for me. The waiter offered to refill Atson's all-you-can-eat shrimp plate, but Atson waved him off.

Once the waiter was gone, Carina set to outlining her drop and pickup plan, showing Atson a couple of Weeping Mountain Valley maps on her wristpiece as visual aids. Atson latched onto it all fast, and soon he was suggesting better drop points and explaining the wind and weather patterns common to the area.

For her part, Carina was doing everything she could to encourage his input, asking questions about flying, leaning in and listening to his anecdotes with what appeared to be genuine fascination. Only a few strands of her long hair were out of the ponytail and framing her face, but she kept sweeping them back and tucking them behind her ears.

Discussing the finer points of his job with Carina and correcting her incorrect assumptions about flying seemed to be giving Atson a great big ego-boner. Probably a penis one as well. He was so engrossed in her being engrossed in him that he didn't ask once why we wanted to be dropped in the middle of the jungle. Throughout their conversation, Atson scooted closer and closer to her until they were sitting side by side, not quite touching.

"So you're saying you can do it," I interrupted, still playing the workaholic partner. "Great, but how much is this going to cost us?"

"Yeah." Carina bit her lip and cast her long lashes down toward the table. "This is kind of embarrassing, but we are on a budget."

"Don't worry about that," Atson said. "I get a salary plus commission on each drop I make working for Dangerous Game, so I don't need to put the hurt on you for my supper. I'll take you out and pick you up if you pay for fuel and add a thousand each way."

Which was probably twice what he was making in commissions.

"Thank you so much!" Carina squeezed his bicep in gratitude. "That would be amazing. You're absolutely hired."

She was good. That retard Nick probably had no idea at all what he was marrying.

≡

AFTER WE SET UP A TIME THE NEXT DAY TO MEET with Atson for our drop and finished our drinks, Carina followed me out of the restaurant. I veered away from the stolen Fedra and headed down the street.

Behind me, her steps faltered. "Where are you going?"

"Trading up," I said, scanning the parked cars for something a little more my class. A custom chopped, toxic-waste-green rat rod on the opposite side of the road caught my eye.

I started the timer on my wristpiece, then crossed the street, keeping an eye out for potential witnesses. The rat rod's doors had been fitted with simple techtumblers. I pressed the victor crystal set in the band of my wristpiece to the techtumbler's faceplate and listened to the static inside the lock as it freaked out.

A second later, the doors unlocked with a muted *clunk*. I opened the driver's side and climbed in.

Carina didn't go to the passenger side. "Do we need a new car?"

"We've been driving that one for a couple days now," I said, opening the e-skeleton key app and starting the download for aftermarket MercyFire ignition locks. "Whoever it belonged to might have come back and reported it stolen."

They probably hadn't, though. There had been barely any accumulation of dust or dirt on the Fedra when we jacked it, which meant it hadn't been sitting in that long-term lot for very long at all.

"What if this belongs to Atson?" she asked, still standing in the street.

I snorted. "Not in his wettest dreams. He's probably driving some mass market piece of shit. Or that cheap excuse for a crotchrocket over there."

The e-skeleton key app beeped a finished notification and I let my wristpiece interface with the ignition. The rat rod screamed like an awakened hogzilla.

I hit the timer on my wristpiece. "Fifty-nine seconds! Jubal, you monster-cocked virtuoso, how do you stand yourself?"

Carina still hadn't gotten in.

"Are you going to stand out there all night waiting for rain, or are you going to get in the car?" I asked.

She got in. We started our drive back to the Glass House in our beautiful new rat rod.

"Is something bothering you?" Carina asked.

"I'm a day away from proving I'm the best thief in the history of the Revived Earth—yet again—by waltzing into an unwaltzable village, and you want to know if something's bothering me?" I grinned and hit the button to put the ragtop down. "Sister, I've never felt better in my whole life."

She was quiet for several blocks. Then, raising her voice to be heard over the wind, she said, "You seem different tonight."

"I'm not."

She didn't contradict me.

I glanced over at her. The wind whipped her ponytail and the face-framing hairs around her head. She was holding the hair back on the left side of her face, away from her cheek.

"What's with the new hairdo?" I asked.

She shrugged. "It's hot down here, and I hate it when my hair sticks to my face."

"Does it bother your scars?"

The wind tore away her answer, so I had to ask, "What?"

"Sometimes," she said louder.

We turned down a traffic-packed street and had to slow to a crawl.

Carina added in a quieter voice, "The acid should have destroyed the nerve endings, but it made them hypersensitive instead. So, sometimes contact bothers them more. Especially when it's hot and humid like this."

I nodded, trying to decide whether she was telling the truth. What would she have to gain by lying about her scars? Maybe sympathy? Pity? But again I couldn't see an endgame in that. And if it was true, then it was a weakness. Why tell me? So I would realize it was true and that she was revealing something about herself, and in turn, feel compelled to reveal something about myself?

"Are you sure you're all right, Van Zandt?" Carina asked. "You've been quiet tonight."

"Still tired," I said. "That freaky Courten gal really wore me out."

The way the scarred corner of Carina's mouth twitched I knew there was a smile on the rest of her face. "I'm sure you've heard the lecture before, but you did use protection, right?"

"Carina, I'm a grown-ass man, of course I used protection. I had a knuckgun within reach the entire time."

She laughed. "I'm serious."

"Me, too." I let off the brake long enough for the rat to roll forward another inch, then stopped again. "Why? Worried about me?"

"Yeah."

My foot slipped off the brake, and I had to stomp on it again before we rolled into the back of the cargo carrier in front of us.

"Well, you shouldn't be." I leaned an arm on the door panel and rested my head in my hand so I could dig my fingernails into the back of my scalp. It didn't help.

Out of the corner of my eye, I saw Carina shrug. "I want everybody I care about to be safe."

"Then why don't you pray for them," I taunted.

"I do."

I sat up, squeezed the rat rod's wheel, and shifted from one side of my butt to the other. "Lot of good it did your dad."

If I hadn't been used to her Carina-pauses by then, I might have thought I'd scored a direct hit with that one. She was quiet for a long time. We'd almost stop-and-goed our way through half a city block before she spoke again.

"Maybe it did," she said.

"Holy fuck," I said, shifting in my seat again, my muscle fibers suddenly crawling with restless fishhooks of energy. "Don't pray to your asshole deity for me, Carina. I can't take that kind of blessing. I like my entrails right where they are."

She didn't say anything to that. She didn't say anything for the remaining two hours we sat in traffic, the thirty second elevator ride, or the short walk to our separate rooms.

It wasn't a thinking silence or an angry silence. I think she was hurt. I think I hurt her.

As soon as I heard Carina's room door close, I checked the security screen, then stepped back into the empty hall to see what sort of nighttime entertainment Giku had to offer.

FIFTEEN_

M Y WRISTPIECE BEEPED, AND I CAME FULL awake.

"Whassat?" a groggy feminine voice asked from over my shoulder. "Time is it?"

The pillows and blankets were scattered around the floor, their white fabric stained orangish-blue by the light pollution coming in through the window wall. I was lying across the hotel room's wide couch instead of on the bed. My arm was hanging off the side, my knuckles brushing the indigo carpet.

My wristpiece beeped again. Two messages. I started to raise my arm to check them.

Soft, sleep-warm breasts and burning thighs moved against my back.

"That your wristpiece or mine?" she mumbled.

I pushed her off. "You're the ko grandmaster. Why don't you use your incredible powers of logic and strategy to figure it out?"

She laughed as if I'd made a really clever joke.

"How about I use my incredible powers of seduction instead?" She ran her hand down my stomach toward my dick.

I elbowed her off me and got out of bed, scanning the room for her clothes.

"Yeah, I was lying about that." I found her button-down shirt, tie, and one high-heeled shoe. "Your pickup lines aren't charming, and your method of seduction is contrived and robotic."

She sat up on the couch, pulling a pillow off the floor to cover herself. "It worked on you."

"They'll make anyone a grandmaster nowadays." I held the clothes out to her. "Get dressed and get out."

"What? Why?"

"Because I tried international ko player and it turns out I don't have an automaton fetish. I like my women capable of expressing emotion. Your ex and I have that in common, I guess."

"I'm not an automaton!"

Her other shoe lay half in the bathroom.

"Could've fooled me," I said as I picked it up.

"I was an excellent lover!" You could see her replay the moves back in her mind and arrive at a concluded victory. "Tonight was everything that's required of a spontaneous sexual encounter!"

Another beep. The reminder notification for unchecked messages.

On the way to the door, my foot caught in her skirt. I kicked it up into my hands.

"What are you doing?" she demanded.

"I already asked you once to leave, but you obviously can't process human speech." I opened the door and tossed her clothes out into the hallway. Her sandal thudded off of the opposite wall.

"You can't do that!" she yelled. "Those are mine!"

"Like I'm going to throw my own shit out of my room. Now get out before I throw you out, too."

A tear ran down her cheek. She stood up and swiped it away.

"I am not robotic," she said. "And I don't have to put up with this kind of treatment."

I held the door for her.

She lifted her chin and walked naked into the hallway as if that would show me.

I let the door swing shut behind her, sick to my stomach.

My wristpiece's message reminder beeped again. Finally alone, I checked it.

CX 00:59:06 *I'll pray for whoever I want.*

CX 00:59:19 *I'm Carina fucking Xiao.*

I threw back my head and laughed.

JVZ 01:06:08 *Want to get some breakfast?*

CX 01:07:08 *It's six a.m. somewhere.*

THE GLASS HOUSE HOTEL'S RESTAURANT wasn't open after midnight, but Carina and I compromised by ordering up to her room and eating in the hall by her door. I got waffles. She got every kind of non-seafood protein on the menu, fried. We both enjoyed a steaming black cup of imported Ad'brum'sarl dark roast.

"This is incredible," Carina said. She took another sip of the coffee. "Like drinking a summer night. I can almost hear the tree frogs."

"Hey, what do you know, the iron stomach has taste buds, too," I said, elbowing her.

She flinched, smiling, and tucked her arm against her side to protect her ribs from follow-up attacks. Apparently Carina fucking Xiao, the Bloodslinger, named knight of the Guild, was ticklish.

"Just because I don't spend all my time complaining doesn't mean I don't recognize good when I taste it," she said.

I broke off a corner of my waffle. "Then taste this."

She did. "Wow."

"Yeah."

"Want any of this?" She indicated her tray.

"All right, let's have some of that bacon."

"There's a hot pepper remoulade to dip it in."

I tried some. "Good God Almighty."

She laughed. "Right?"

"Okay, sister, plates in the middle," I said, arranging the trays between us longwise and turning to face her. "This is a breakfast buffet now."

"Best idea you've had all day." Carina crossed her legs and spun around on her butt to face the food. She reached over and pulled off another bite of my waffle.

We sat out there eating and joking until the food was gone. Every now and then a late-night reveler would give us bewildered looks as they stumbled past on the way to their room.

When we were done, I stacked our empty plates and trays together and sat them next to the door across from Carina's, then I leaned back against the wall next to her.

She stretched, arching her back and moaning low in her throat. "That was exactly what I wanted."

"Same here, except now I'm about half a blink from passing out," I said.

"Same." She checked her wristpiece. "Plenty of time. We're not leaving here until eight."

I knew it wasn't what she meant, but I went for the joke anyway. "If you're inviting me back to your room, Bloodslinger, I accept, but I should warn you up front that I'm exhausted. I mean, I'll give it a shot, but it's not going to be my best work."

Carina smiled and stood up. "Good thing that wasn't an invitation, then."

"If you want to cuddle, I guess…"

"Good night, Jubal," she said, unlocking her door.

"Your loss." I shrugged. "I'm a world-class cuddler."

"Go get some rest in your five-star bed. Tomorrow's going to be a long one."

THAT NIGHT, AS I WAS DOZING OFF, I IMAGINED me and Carina playing in the jungle alongside Courten's river—except in this scenario, it was bright yellow daylight and she and I were little kids. We screeched and laughed and chased each other around the trees and threw rocks into muddy water.

It wasn't a dream, though. I was still awake, at least a little bit. When my entire body twitched in reality to catch my child-self from an imagined fall, the memory of that make-believe scene stuck in my throat and stomach like a poisoned knife.

I got up, went to the bathroom, and splashed water on my face. Then I stared into the dark brown eyes in the mirror, inspecting the ring of black around the irises until I was sure I wasn't going to go back into the bedroom, throw the valuables safe through the wall of windows, and follow it out.

SIXTEEN_

WE LEFT THE HOTEL THE NEXT MORNING WITH thirty minutes to spare, made a quick stop at a camping and outdoor supply store for camping and outdoor supplies, then found the Dangerous Game resort.

Atson and another guy were waiting for us at the helipad.

"This is Dax," Atson said. "He's going to be our spotter. I can't check your rope or make sure you're ready to jump while I'm hovering, so he'll do the final checks and give you all the signals. Dax knows everything there is to know about rope work. You're in good hands."

Neither Dax nor Atson seemed surprised that Carina was decked out in jungle camo with knives strapped to her thighs, pockets full of backup knuckgun magazines, and replacement saw chain wrapped around her fists and wrists like jewelry, but Atson tugged his goatee at my brightly-colored tourist shirt and khaki pants and shot Dax an amused look.

"Let me guess," Atson said to Carina. "John here is going to distract the prey while you shoot it?"

He and Dax guffawed at his joke. I laughed good-naturedly and fingered the throat-pin in my wristpiece band.

When the hilarity died down, Carina asked, "Are we ready to go?"

"Almost. Got to do the lecture." Atson held up a harness and went off on a practiced spiel. "Just slip this on and pull tight here, here, and here. Do not—repeat, *do not*—set your harness down somewhere and lose it while you're out. If you lose it, you won't have anything to hook onto when I come to pick you up."

We each took a harness and pulled them on like an extra layer of underwear, then pulled the straps tight. Atson looked a little disappointed at how quickly and easily Carina got hers on and adjusted. He'd probably been hoping to spend some time feeling around her crotch under the pretense of helping.

"The drop is a simple rappel," Atson continued. "The pickup will be a simple winch back into the chopper—*if* you don't lose your harnesses. Any questions?"

I raised my hand. "I'm not clear on the harnesses, RE: level of importance."

Atson gave me a flat look, then turned to Carina to see if she had any questions. She didn't. This wasn't her first rappel. It wasn't mine, either, but I didn't feel it necessary to share that information with the group.

With the lecture out of the way, Carina and Atson spent a few minutes transferring the fuel money into his account—the rest she would transfer after he picked us up—and then we climbed into the helicopter.

The cockpit was a one-seater, just big enough for Atson, but the bay, where Dax, Carina, and I sat, was made to hold several hunters and whatever big game they had bagged.

Donut rings, pulleys, and tackle threaded with black cord hung from the roof. A winch was set into the floor. Dax spent a few minutes assigning Carina and me headphones, ropes, gloves, and descenders, then showed us the guide hand and brake hand maneuvers. We sat on the edge of the bay with our feet on the landing gear, did a couple of dry runs, then we were ready to go.

Atson started up the helicopter, and we lifted off.

THE CANOPY OF SOAM'S RAINFOREST IS NINETY percent vine, ten percent tree, sort of like a giant net with a few holes in it, through which you could see almost all the way to the ground. Once we made it over the Weeping Mountains and into the valley, Atson brought us down closer to the vegetation net, looking for the specific hole he and Carina had decided on the day before. I kept an eye out for dark ponds that might match the one the Courten witch had drawn for us, but couldn't see anything through the canopy cover.

Finally, the helicopter stopped its horizontal momentum and hovered over a huge clearing.

Atson's voice came through our headphones, "Over drop zone."

"Drop zone check," Dax responded. He leaned out and glanced around the clearing below. "Clear. Equipment check." He jerked on my harness, the ring my rope was looped through in the floor, the descender, nodded at my gloves, then said, "Hunter one clear for drop." He checked Carina over in the same efficient manner, then nodded. "Hunter two clear for drop."

"Go in five," Atson said.

Carina took her headphones off and handed them back. She sent her bag zipping down the rope first, then sat on the floor of the helicopter, put her feet on the landing gear, and waited.

"Go, hunter two," Dax yelled, slapping her on the shoulder.

Carina jumped. She hit the ground, ran backward until the rope was free, then signaled that she was clear. Textbook execution.

Dax reeled in Carina's rope, then nodded at me. I handed him my headphones, tossed my bag down the rope, sat with my feet on the landing gear, and waited. My heart was pounding, and a wild grin had spread across my face.

Over the noise from the blades, I could just barely hear Dax yell, "Go, hunter one," as he slapped me on the back.

I jumped.

I don't screw around showboating on the 'Shan because the potential to end up with a face that looks like ground meat is too high. Gotta protect the moneymaker. Additionally, with the number of variables I don't have control over on any given road, the risk of death greatly outweighs the reward of a couple seconds' thrill. But in a situation like this, when I don't have any other ingress options, and the variables I don't have control over have been cut down to just one or two, I love a good adrenaline rush.

The wind washed over my face and riffled through my hair as I shot toward the ground. A laugh bubbled up out of my chest. I could've dropped forever.

My sneakers slammed down, and I put an arm over my face and ran backward to unthread the rope. When the rope was free, Dax reeled it back in.

Within a matter of seconds, the helicopter was gone.

Carina was crouched a few yards away, digging her knuckgun out of her bag. She felt me watching her and raised her head.

The smile lit up her whole face. "It's never bad, is it?"

"Never," I said.

For the next couple of seconds we just stood there grinning like idiots together.

≡

WE COULDN'T BE SURE HOW RELIABLE THE laptic grid would be inside the mountain valley, so Carina and I both checked our position on our wristpieces. The wristpieces agreed. If they were wrong, then they were at least both the same amount of wrong. We synced our wristpieces, shouldered our bags, and set off toward the marker Carina had made on the nav app in the dark pond area.

The jungle grew denser as we walked, until Carina had to take out the machete she'd bought that morning and start chopping. There wasn't much to talk about or much motivation to do more than huff, puff, and sweat. Bloodsuckers of various and sundry sizes came out to investigate us, looking for—and finding—weak spots in our greasy coating of repellant. The branches, vines, and brambles that Carina didn't waste her energy cutting down because they weren't a direct obstacle to continuing scraped, scratched, and pulled at us, occasionally opening up new holes for the bloodsuckers to exploit. The air, which had been a blanket of humidity in Courten, was now a boiling cauldron.

It occurred to me several times during the walk that this was the reason I was a creature of luxury—the jungle sucks. But every time I looked down at the nav screen on my wristpiece and saw that blinking marker a few steps closer, I got more excited.

"What are you talking about back there?" Carina asked, pausing for a second to swipe her long sleeve across her forehead. The tactical fiber blend soaked up the sweat and made it disappear.

"Just reminding myself how awesome I am," I said between breaths.

"Any particular reason?"

I pointed to the marker on my wristpiece. "Unwaltzable village." I pointed to myself. "Currently waltzing."

"Best thief in the history of the Revived Earth," Carina said.

"You're damn right I am."

She started chopping at the undergrowth again. "That's why I hired you."

I considered it. At this point, it was almost a certainty that the job was legit and everything Carina had said so far relating to getting revenge on those brujahs was the truth as she saw it. For someone to have okayed the time, cost, and energy sunk into setting up a sting operation this elaborate and disguise it to this depth was implausible, even for the Guild.

But I liked knowing that Carina agreed that I was the best thief in the history of the Revived Earth. And she would know that I liked it and that my ego would want to believe her when she said so.

But then what about all that nonsense about her scars being hypersensitive in this humidity, and admitting that she was wrong about the fix-it witch? What about on the drive to Courten when she was acting like a suicidal psycho with nothing to gain but shutting me up or killing us both, and all those times I had surprised her into laughing?

A bloodsucker as big around as my wrist landed on my forearm. Before it could shove its proboscis through the muscle and into my bone, I smacked it. The bulbous thorax splattered gore all over my arm. I wiped my hand on the back of Carina's bag.

She didn't look back.

"You think this is the first time someone's wiped something on me and thought I wouldn't notice?" she called over her shoulder. "I'll get you back."

I smiled. "Just keep in mind that if you do something bad, I'm going to do something worse."

"Oh, I expect you to."

For a second I was sure I could hear two little kids' high-pitched laughing, but it was just something off in the jungle shrieking. That poisoned knife slipped into my gut again as I watched Carina hacking away at the greenery.

I didn't want her to be manipulating me. I wanted this to be real.

≡

AT THE FIRST INDICATION OF SUNSET, WE stopped. Carina made a fire and boiled water for our supper, then sharpened her machete on a whetstone while I set up the hammock tents we'd gotten from that outdoor supplies store.

According to the nav app, we'd made it less than ten miles, but we were both exhausted.

"That leaves us just three or four miles to go tomorrow," Carina said, handing over my reconstituted gruel pack. "We can find their village, spend some time scouting, then come in after dark."

I eyed my gruel, then upended the package and swallowed it all in one gulp before I could taste it. The hot goop traced a burning trail down my esophagus into my stomach. Because that's what this trip needed, more heat.

"Now you're thinking like somebody with some common sense," I said. "Stealth is hot. Just look at me."

She snorted and scooped a bite out of her package with the little wooden spoon that had come glued to the side. "How was the food, creature of luxury?"

"Don't quit your day job."

She laughed.

I stood and stretched, then went off a ways to take a leak. When I came back, I climbed into my hammock tent.

"Whoever set up the tents, now," I said, wiggling my shoulders and butt to get comfortable,

"That guy's some kind of genius. He didn't have much to work with, but he really pulled it off."

Through the window netting, I could see Carina shaking her head, trying to hold back a grin as she ate.

I shut my eyes and tried to hold onto that image. Even without the white noise of an air conditioner, I was asleep in no time.

IT WAS PITCH BLACK WHEN I OPENED MY EYES again, and rain was pouring onto my tent. Our fire must have been doused. I strained my ears, trying to hear past the downpour and jungle night noises for what had woken me up.

"Van Zandt!" Carina hissed.

By the sound of her voice, she was right outside my hammock tent.

"What?" I whispered.

"Don't move, okay?"

"What? Why not?"

"There's something big circling us."

I listened to the constant crackling and popping of rain on leaves, trying to hear what she heard. Guild knights came standard with hyperaural upgrades, possibly even noise-filtration nowadays. There was no way my unmodified eardrums could compete with hers.

"Are you sure?" I whispered.

"Yeah. You didn't hear it growl?"

"I was asleep until just a second ago."

"Are you serious? It was close by."

The story Carina's mother had told her about the woman and kids being eaten by black oncas loomed in my brain. "What do you think it is?"

"Shh."

I focused as hard as I could, but still couldn't make anything out. The rain was too loud.

If something bad was going to happen, my flame kigao should have been warning me. Maybe whatever animal Carina had heard had already moved on.

"Do you still hear—"

"Shh!"

Undergrowth crashed, and Carina's knuckgun went off twice. Carina grunted as if she'd been punched in the stomach. Something huge smashed onto my tent, caving it in and pinning me to the ground. I thrashed and shoved, on the edge of blind panic. I needed a knife. I couldn't find the tent zipper. I couldn't get the thing off of me. It was dead weight, hotter even than the soupy night air. But it wasn't moving.

Maybe one of Carina's shots had killed it. I tried kicking and elbowing, but I couldn't get free. The thing shuddered.

I froze.

It shuddered *in rhythm.*

It was laughing.

Out of all the creatures in the Soami rainforest that can laugh or mimic laughter, only one had promised to get me back twice now.

That was why the kigao hadn't woken me up. I wrenched one hand out from between the dead weight of the thing and my chest, then dug my fingers into the ribs of the thing.

Carina wasn't even bothering to silence the giggles now.

"Slime whore!" I yelled, smacking her through the tent with my free hand. "Evil, siltbrained, parasite-fucker!"

She rolled off the tent, still laughing like some sort of insane holostar villain.

I ripped open my tent's zipper. Rain dripped onto my head and shoulders, surprisingly cold for such a hot night. Water was already pooling in the spot she'd vacated.

Carina was sitting cross-legged in front of my tent door, still laughing, seemingly oblivious to the water and mud that was probably soaking into the ass of her cammies.

I reached out and shoved her. She rolled gracefully feet over head until she was kneeling a body length away, probably in the wet ashes that had been our fire.

"Careful, Jubal," she said, a grinning upward lilt to her voice. "Knuckgun's still loaded."

"What kind of psycho uses live rounds for a practical joke?" I yelled. I still sounded angry, but inside I was laughing hysterically as a little girl with a wide pink scar on her cheek chased me through the trees.

Another round of giggles bubbled out of her throat at my question. "What kind of psycho would bring blanks on a revenge mission?"

"And you ruined my tent!" I jerked the nano-endoskeleton. It popped back into shape.

"Your tent's fine. You should've heard your voice. 'What?! What was it?!'"

"You're a child," I said.

I crawled back into my hammock and zipped the tent shut. It was a poor substitute for a door slam, an undignified two-part zip, but it made Carina laugh harder, so I think she got the intent.

In the darkness of my tent, I held my stomach and laughed until my throat hurt from the effort it took to stay silent. Being friends with a psycho was fun. And my skin was still warm where she'd been pressed against me.

SEVENTEEN_

I
N SPITE OF HER MIDDLE-OF-THE-NIGHT PRANK, Carina was up before dawn and back to focusing single-mindedly on the revenge at hand. In the stormy gray-blue light, I could see that her tactical shirt and pants were covered in mud, but she didn't seem to mind. The rain was still pouring down, so she probably figured the mud would either be washed away or lend her extra concealment.

We packed everything we might possibly need during the day into our pockets, left the tents and our bags behind, then headed out.

The rain had slowed to a drizzle and the jungle had brightened to overcast when we set foot on the banks of the first dark pond an hour later. We crouched in the vegetation for a few minutes, watching the muddy area surrounding the pond for anything that might betray it as the water source for a magically locked-down brujah village. Corpse candles danced across the surface of the black water, and dead faces stared back out of the depths, their hair billowing out around them, but nothing else moved, and neither Carina nor I felt it *like a sodee pop*, so we moved on.

The farther into the dark ponds area we traveled, the more the undergrowth thinned out, until finally

Carina was able to put her machete away. We stopped to surveil six more dark ponds along the way, none of which caused any sodee pop sensations or showed signs of regular human usage.

The ambient light grew brighter and brighter until the drizzle broke off. The sun peeked through the trees for a few seconds before disappearing again, but the black water of the dark ponds never changed hue.

It was well after noon when we came to the eighth pond. It was significantly larger than the rest of the ponds we'd come across so far, and runoff from a huge carrion cypress was pouring into it like a waterfall, vomiting up black mist and distorting the corpse candles on the surface and the dead faces' hair under the surface.

Carina settled into a squat a few yards back from the tree line. I hunkered down beside her.

Time passed.

Nothing moved.

Carina looked at me. I knew what she was thinking. This had to be it. Look at the mist, for crying out loud. And the tree? A coven of aguas brujahs couldn't pick a more thematically consistent place to set up shop.

I mouthed *Closer?* and shrugged.

She nodded.

We crawled to the sweeping cover of a willow on the pond bank. I went to pull myself up into a crouch again, but something cold poured down my nose and into my eyes, tiny bubbles fizzing and popping. I blinked and scrubbed at my eyes as water welled up in them, my tear ducts trying to flush the acidic foreign substance out before it did any damage.

When I looked up, Carina was doing the same thing.

And over her shoulder, I saw it.

The aguas brujahs' village was primitive and tribal-looking, even compared to a puddle like Courten. The only structures were lean-tos made of mud, leaves, and the long bones of prehistoric or still-undiscovered creatures, with woven mats strewn across the mud floors for sitting and sleeping on. Altars were set up in the center of each hut with a clay bowl of black water as the lynchpin. The huts—and therefore the altars at each one's epicenter—were set up in a semicircle around the far bank of the dark pond to most effectively harness its energy.

Brujahs were going about their day, lying, sitting, walking around, talking, eating, or cooking over the big village bonfire whose smoke we could now see rising up toward the jungle canopy. I counted at least a dozen adults, maybe three or four kids. If not for the extra mud and their out-of-date but immaculate Guild Ministries to Soam clothing, I could have mistaken any one of them for the standard dirty homeless person or mutie.

I turned to Carina to see what she wanted to do next, but our silent confab was interrupted. My wristpiece vibrated four times in quick succession. A local emergency alert signal. Carina's must have been vibrating, too, because she frowned down at it.

I grinned. That could've been bad. I hadn't even thought to remind her to silence hers this morning before we left camp.

Across the pond, all over the brujahs' village, wristpieces were beeping the four-tone emergency alert.

My wristpiece vibrated again, demanding I check the alert right now. I relented just to shut it up.

Carina's Guild file photo popped up on my screen followed by scrolling text.

Emdoni Guild Knight Carina Xiao, daughter of Emdoni Guild Knight Cormac Xiao, Child Butcher. Wanted for multiple murders. Believed to be in the Giku area. ARMED AND EXTREMELY DANGEROUS. Any information or sightings respond immediately to this message.

Beside me, Carina was glaring down at her wristpiece. She raised her head, looking across the dark pond to the brujahs, most of whom were in the process of reading the same emergency alert.

Then she looked at me. Her eyes were a lighter green than I'd ever seen them, the color of glacial swamp ice.

Before, going in under the cover of night would have given her the upper hand. Now, every minute that passed would allow the brujahs to dig in and protect themselves that much more effectively. She had to utilize her advantage while she still had one.

All of this she told me with a look.

I couldn't see any alternative. I nodded.

Across the pond, a brujah jumped to her feet and opened her mouth as if she were about to address the coven.

Carina pulled her knuckgun and shot the brujah in the back of the head.

The Bloodslinger had come to town.

≡

SIR CARINA XIAO, THE BLOODSLINGER, HAD received her name in a ceremony that followed her second active rotation on Emden's eastern front—what Guild knights lovingly call "over east"—and preceded her seventeenth birthday.

Shortly after she'd arrived over east, her patrol company had been ambushed by pagan raiders. Two of her company were killed outright. But Carina fucking Xiao and the remaining members of her company didn't just unhorse and kill the raiders who had ambushed them. They unhorsed and killed the raiders, and then Carina fucking Xiao led her company in tracking the raiders back to their village of origin, slaying everything breathing, and burning the place to the ground.

The record keeper of her patrol company had set his wristpiece to record as soon as they were ambushed, so if you've got an untraceable infoserve app and the time to dig through the Guild's files, you can watch the whole thing. I did after making it back to Emden because Carina had never gotten around to telling me how she got her name.

By the time she had finished leveling the raiders' village, Carina was soaked in what was probably equal parts blood and sweat. It was running freely down her arms and face, dripping off her shortsword like water, and the chain-driven saw on the edge of her knuckgun's guard threw red mist up into the air.

At the very end, just before the record keeper stops the recording, he takes a visual head count of the remaining knights in his company to send in ahead of their return. When those last few seconds of footage get to Carina, you can see very clearly as she raises her sword arm, swipes her wrist across her face, then slings it out to the side, shedding bright red droplets of blood against the backdrop of a pale sunrise.

Which is all to say that, when it comes to laying waste to a village, Sir Carina Xiao, the Bloodslinger, has a history of not messing around.

☰

ONLY A FEW OF THE AGUAS BRUJAHS IN THE village panicked when Carina shot that first one. The rest remained calm, which made that first couple seconds of bloodshed eerily quiet.

Carina picked off three more of the brujahs from her spot beside me. She was going for the ones who looked as if they were mounting a defense.

While she did that, a pair of brujahs ran for opposite ends of the semicircle hut setup. They swept their arms out wide, still running, then brought them together and dove into the black water of the pond, perfectly synchronized. Their dives didn't even make a splash.

"The electricity is about to go out," my flame kigao said, crouching beside me.

"Shit." I looked at Carina to see if she'd noticed.

"Get down," she said.

She flipped the safety on a shrapgrenade, hit the button, and winged it over the pond into the village. She dropped to a crouch and covered her head with her arms.

The surface of the black water rippled. Nothing had exploded yet.

"Carina."

"The electricity is about to go out."

The shrapgrenade detonated with a *pling*ing sound like metal hail. Bits of shrapnel ripped through lean-tos and brujah flesh alike. Now they were screaming.

Carina sprang out of the crouch and sprinted for the village.

Waves in the dark pond flowed *toward* the explosion.

"The electricity—"

"Carina, the pond!"

Carina skidded to a stop, her boots making trails in the sandy mud of the bank.

The mist coming off of the carrion cypress's waterfall shifted, rolling toward her. The black waves of the pond crashed against the shore, then folded back in on themselves, stacking and boiling until a water monster as tall as the cypress stood in the wet mud of the pond floor. Dead faces twisted and screamed with rage inside the creature's foamy black skin.

Carina covered the brujahs in the village with her knuckgun and whipped out her machete with her free hand.

The water monster flowed onto the bank. Carina whirled away. The monster crashed its fist down where she'd been standing. Carina chopped through its arm. Oily black water soaked into the dirt.

The monster howled with the furious voices of the restless dead. In place of the arm Carina had chopped, the monster grew a huge morning star of spiked black ice. It swung at her. She rolled away. It swung again. She rolled again, this time up to one knee, and squeezed off three shots at the monster's head. The bullets punched through, then sheared off at odd angles, leaving spikes of black ice in their wake.

In the village, seemingly forgotten by the monster and Carina, four of the remaining aguas brujahs were at their altars, gulping down the liquid from their clay bowls.

"Now, what are the odds that they're just very thirsty?" I asked my kigao.

She looked at me with those burning blood eyes. "The electricity is—"

I nodded. "That's what I thought."

The drinking brujahs returned their clay bowls carefully to their altars, then dropped to their knees, arms lifted to the sky.

Thunder boomed overhead, and the rain clouds all shot their load at the same time. As one, the four kneeling brujahs flowed to their feet, shouting in a dialect I couldn't understand. Their arms shook with strain.

The water monster swelled as the rain added to its volume. It had two ice arms now. Carina must've chopped the other one off while I was watching the brujahs.

Bedrock cracked as the water monster slammed its twin black ice morning stars into the ground where Carina had been standing. I lost sight of her for a second, then she somersaulted out from between the monster's legs. Dark pond water splashed, and the monster tipped off balance. She'd sliced through one of its legs.

An ice pillar covered in razor spikes sprouted in the leg's place. Carina darted back in before the monster could turn around. The last liquid leg collapsed and streamed across the saturated bank. An ice pillar took its place.

Carina jerked another shrapgrenade from her cammies. She came in from the side this time, ducking under a powerful morning star swing. She used the spikes on one of the monster's ice pillar legs to run up its side. Her fist and forearm disappeared into its chest. She leapt free and hit the ground running.

A second later, one of the synchrodiving brujahs hurled herself from the center of the monster's chest. The left half of the monster's body dropped, limp without its animator.

The other synchrodiving brujah got her head and arm free of the water monster, but that was it.

The water monster exploded from the inside out, firing shrapnel, brujah meat, and ice shards as big as scythes in all directions.

I hit the ground behind the willow. Splintered wood and bits of ice fell on my back and shoulders. When I looked up again, the willow's whips were tattered and scraggly.

Black mist swirled around the pond and village, a howling whirlpool of the revenants the brujahs had been syphoning their magical energy from. There was no more water in the dark pond to hold them in check.

A shot cut through the revenant mist and took the remaining synchrodiving brujah down. Carina spun, trying to get the next brujah in her knuckgun's sights.

With a sound like a gasp, all of the revenants sucked inward at once. Where the four drinking brujahs had been shouting up at the sky now stood four many-tentacled creatures of dense black shadow.

Carina fired. Her knuckgun's slide locked back.

The shadow creature she'd shot absorbed the bullet. The air rattled, then drops of molten slag hissed through the rain toward Carina.

She whirled away, ejecting her knuckgun's empty magazine and slapping a full one home.

The shadow creatures poured themselves across the ground like water, surrounding her. She spun and shot and spun and shot some more. They puked her melted bullets back at her in a burning spray.

I got to my feet and ran. Behind me, I heard the chain-driven saw on Carina's knuckgun scream to life. I stuck to the edge of the tree line, keeping the shadow creatures in my sight at all times. They were closing in on Carina. Every now and then I caught a flash of her at the center, lashing out with the machete and her knuckgun's saw, but for the most part all I could see were thrashing tentacles.

The village came up on my right, and I slipped between the lean-tos. The first two altars I found were topped off with clay bowls full of dark pond water. I jumped over a brujah corpse and kept going. The next altar's bowl was empty.

I stomped the bowl into bloody red shards, then kicked over the altar. Baby finger bones scattered in the mud.

One of the shadow creatures went up in a *whoosh* of white mist and black flame. The brujah at the center screamed and dropped to the ground, trying to put out the spirit fire as it burned her alive.

I didn't wait around to see what happened next. I heard the knuckgun, I could guess. I had more important things to do than stand around watching.

I found the next empty clay bowl altar and wrecked it. Another shadow monster *whoosh*ed into mist and flame. As soon as she could see the brujah at the center, Carina shot.

One of the two remaining shadow creature's tentacles finally got hold of Carina's arm and jerked her toward its empty blackness. Carina drove the machete into its heart. The shadow creature tried to absorb the machete, but Carina held fast.

I tore up another empty-bowl altar. The shadow creature that Carina wasn't elbow deep in *whoosh*ed, and its brujah fell to the ground, howling.

Carina yelled as she fought to keep the rest of her body and what was left of the machete from sinking into the black nothingness at the heart of the last shadow creature.

The next three altars I passed had full bowls. Only one lean-to in the village left. I ran for it.

I heard Carina fire her knuckgun into the shadow creature, maybe to buy herself a little time.

I kicked the last altar as I ran, scattering broken bits of pottery and finger bones. Both crunched and squished into the mud under my shoes as I decelerated to a stop.

From behind me came a *whoosh,* then the slick sound of a blade being pulled from flesh. I turned around. Carina was bent over, wiping the blood from her machete on a brujah's bright red shirt. The black flames of spirit fire sputtered and died as the brujah's soul fled her corpse.

Carina looked up at me, chest heaving as she worked to catch her breath, and shook her head. "I can't think of anything."

"Huh?"

"To say," she breathed. She pointed her machete at the face of the brujah she had just pulled it from. "She's the bitch who killed my dad, and I can't think of anything cool to say."

I cackled. "Me neither."

EIGHTEEN_

I T ONLY TOOK US A COUPLE OF MINUTES TO TRACK THE kids and the last two living brujahs to the cave where they'd hidden out when the shooting began. Without hesitating, Carina put a bullet in both brujahs' heads, then one in each of the kids'.

I scratched at my scraped collarbone. "What was that thing you said earlier about not wanting to be the cause of innocent blood getting spilled?"

"You don't leave survivors," she said. When she looked at me, the slivers of glacial swamp ice were still frozen in her irises. "If that brujah who killed Dad had killed me, too, everyone in this village would still be alive. If my dad and his company had taken out the rest of the Soam force during the war—kids or not—that brujah never would have come for him."

I grinned as ice water trickled down my spine. I'd done it again, gotten caught up in all the fun and games and forgotten that I was dealing with a dangerous animal. Predator, not pet.

"You would make a great serial killer," I told Carina. "Of course, with that level of efficiency, you'd put yourself out of a job in about a year."

Ξ

ON OUR WALK BACK TO THE DECIMATED BRUJAH village, Carina's shoulders slumped and her head sagged with exhaustion.

The rain poured on.

"You don't want to just head back to camp?" I asked her.

She shook her head. "Got to get something first. You can go back without me if you want."

I shrugged. The undamaged components from those altars could probably bring in some serious money on the analog black market, especially considering the fate of the brujahs who'd built them. No sense in letting all that just rot out here in the jungle when I could be making bank off of it.

The ice from the water monster hadn't melted, but the carrion cypress's runoff was flowing into the dark pond again, refilling it. The brujahs in the village were lying where we'd left them. They had paled, bloated, and begun to disintegrate like corpses left in the rain for weeks rather than half an hour.

Carina ignored the bodies and began searching the lean-tos. I busied myself taking pictures of the altars, making sure to get artful shots of the carnage in the background. Then I packed up as many of the bowls and bones as I could carry.

Carina had paused in her search. She was watching me.

"What?" I said. "You have to figure at least a couple of these bowls are going to break in transit. You know how careless international baggage movers are. I can't fence broken pottery, Carina. That would be terrible for business."

"We both know you don't care about the money," she said.

I smiled. "That's adorable. You think you're a mind-reader now."

Carina didn't argue, just went back to searching in and around the lean-tos.

A few minutes later, she came up with a hardhead catfish skull impaled on a pristine thornknife. She jerked the thornknife out and stuck it in her belt. Then she hefted the catfish skull in her hand, bouncing it around on her fingertips until its crucifix faced her. One of its spines was missing.

"This is the catfish head Dad gave Mom when he came back from Soam," she said, tracing the rounded edge of the missing spine with her thumb. "I knocked it off the shelf roughhousing with Mom when I was a kid—broke off the spine and made this scuff mark on the side. I knew I saw it earlier, but I was so focused on that pond monster…"

"Now that's a trophy," I said, pointing one of my clay bowls at it. "Kind of makes you wish you hadn't traded your fish head off to Re Suli, huh?"

"I'm too tired to play this with you right now, Van Zandt," Carina said. She stood up, cradling the catfish skull to her hip with one hand. The other hand she stuck out to me. "Thanks for taking out those altars. You probably saved my life."

I dismissed her hand with a wave of a clay bowl. "I couldn't have you dying when we were this close to payment. Dead man's switch, remember?"

The way she smiled then was too small to be impeded by her scars. She lifted her wristpiece and punched in some commands.

"The switch is off. The money's in your account to stay," she said when she was done. "You more than earned it."

"You get what you pay for," I said, shooting her with the clay bowl version of a finger gun.

≡

IT WAS STILL RAINING WHEN WE MADE IT BACK TO camp. Neither of us wanted to put forth the effort to get a fire going for water-boiling and gruel-reconstituting, so we both took a QalORun bar and slogged into our hammock tents.

I got naked, toweled off with some of my dry clothes, put on some shorts, and scarfed my food.

"Head to the clearing first thing in the morning?" Carina called across camp.

"Yeah." I carefully wrapped each bowlful of bones in dry clothing and nestled them in my bag. "Think Atson will show up with a chopper full of SecOps?"

I couldn't hear Carina's sigh over the constant hiss of raindrops on my tent, but I heard its remainder in her voice when she answered. "We'll burn that rolling log bridge if we come to it."

I smiled and crawled into my hammock. "Goodnight, Carina."

"Goodnight, Jubal."

NINETEEN_

THE NEXT DAY THE RAIN DISAPPEARED. IN ITS place settled a heat so intense that we could actually see the steam rising from the leaves and moss as we hiked. We used up our entire supply of water purification tablets that morning trying to replace the gallons of water leaking out of our pores, and still neither of us had to stop for a single potty break.

For the most part, we were able to stick to the trail we'd taken into the dark pond area, but the rainstorm had brought down new tangles of vines and branches, so Carina put her machete back to work.

When we stopped to risk our colons on some unpurified water and rest around noon, we checked our wristpieces' nav screens.

"Probably two hours left," Carina said. "I'm going to set off the pickup beacon and send him an ETA."

I nodded and wiped my sweat-soaked shirt across my sweat-soaked face. Surprise, surprise, it didn't help.

"Ready?" Carina asked, standing up.

"And raring." I popped to my feet and carefully shouldered my bag. "Let's go find out if Atson fucked us over."

≡

THE TIMING TURNED OUT TO BE PERFECT. JUST before we made it to the drop point, we started hearing the rhythmic *whump* of helicopter blades in the distance.

A wide smile stretched across my face, and renewed energy rushed through my veins. We were almost there. Carina was grinning, too. We jogged the rest of the way to the clearing and stopped just under the cover of the trees to put on our harnesses.

The Dangerous Game trademarked helicopter swung into the open sky overhead. Carina and I spread out to get different visual angles on the bay.

Dax leaned out and dropped a line. I couldn't see anyone else up in there with him.

"What do you think?" I yelled at Carina over the wind.

She had drawn her knuckgun.

"Looks like they're alone from here," she yelled back.

"Same here."

We sprinted to the rope, getting under the belly of the helicopter so that anyone inside who wanted to shoot us would have to lean out. Dax was still the only one in sight. Carina stood guard with her knuckgun while I hooked my harness on and waved up at him. Dax gave the rope a jerk to make sure it was attached, then leaned back into the bay.

The winch lifted me slowly and steadily off my feet. I grabbed the rope to stay upright. At the top, I climbed onto the landing gear and Dax helped me into the bay. I unhooked, and he tossed the rope back down to Carina.

Nothing seemed to have changed from our first drop. Either they had ignored the emergency alert on Carina, deleted it without reading, or all of the SecOps were waiting for us back at the resort. Atson might even have dismissed the alert without thinking about it. The sterile Guild file photo the authorities had sent out didn't look anything like the beautiful, playful woman who'd met Atson at the Giku dinner club, even with the scars. First impressions were hard for most people to shake.

I carefully set my bag full of delicate brujah pottery far away from the door, then came back to look out.

Dax had started the winch. Carina was ascending, one hand on the rope and one hand hidden behind her.

She asked me the SecOps question with a twitch of her eyebrows. I shook my head. Her obscured hand moved, tucking the knuckgun into the back of her pants, then joined her other hand on the rope.

"The electricity is about to go out," my flame kigao whispered, touching my shoulder.

My head snapped up. A shiny, mud-dauber-black chopper came into view a few dozen yards away, pointing its many-barreled mounted minicannon at us. The Dangerous Game chopper shook with turbulence, then leveled out.

"DGR-17," a VoxAmp blared from the black chopper. "BE ADVISED THAT YOU ARE TRANSPORTING WANTED MURDERER CARINA

XIAO. RETURN XIAO TO THE GROUND IMMEDIATELY OR YOU WILL BE TREATED AS HOSTILE."

Carina was still five or six yards from the bay. Below her, uniformed SecOps were flooding the clearing. She drew her knuckgun again, craning her neck to get a better view of the ground.

Beside me, Dax's mouth hung open. He looked paralyzed with shock. In the cockpit, Atson was speaking as fast as he could into his headset.

"NEGATIVE, DGR-17." The butchered Soami Anglish coming over the VoxAmp deepened with frustration. "XIAO IS CLASSIFIED EXTREMELY DANGEROUS. RETURN XIAO TO THE GROUND IMMEDIATELY OR WE WILL OPEN FIRE."

To prove that they were serious, the SecOps' gunner started to spin the minicannon's barrels.

Atson glanced over his shoulder at Dax and me. In spite of his cushy job in Giku, it was obvious that he couldn't make peace with tossing one of his countrywomen to the Soami dogs. He would rather try running and get us all killed.

"FINAL WARNING, DGR-17. RETURN XIAO TO THE—"

I leaned out and looked down.

At some point during the initial turbulence, Atson had been forced to yield the airspace over the clearing to the SecOps chopper. We were over jungle now.

Carina was only two yards from the landing gear. She reached up at me with her free hand.

Without even thinking about it, I grabbed one of the straps in the bay and reached for her.

She smiled, relieved.

That's when the final bit of the knot unraveled and the poisoned knife hit home.

All of the handling other people together, all of the flirting and joking and pretending to be friends, all of the vulnerability and humility and loneliness and leading on—it had all been preparation for a moment like this. She'd been conditioning me so that when I had to face the choice—save my own skin or try to save her and take myself down with her—I wouldn't even think about it. She had tricked me into believing that we were linked, these unique beings in a world full of siltbrains who couldn't understand us, two fires that burned too hot, consuming the planet in search of an intellectual equal—*I'm like you and we are in agreement*—a team, a we, Carina and me versus the world. But there was no we. There was only Carina and her human safety net, her get-home guarantee, one Jubal fucking Van Zandt. She'd handled me, and I'd made it so easy. I saw it happening and I went along willingly anyway, just like one of my father's victims.

The only person who can catch you is you, his voice rang through my head.

A laugh slipped out from between my clenched teeth. Instead of grabbing Carina's hand, I jerked my hand back. Her dark brows scrunched together in confusion as I stood up.

I waved at the SecOps minicannon's gunner and gave him the *Just a sec* motion, then leaned back into the bay and lifted the wicked-looking hunting knife from Dax's belt.

I leaned back out.

Carina's eyes went wide when she saw it. "What are you doing?!"

I didn't answer. She knew.

"Jubal!"

"Nice touch, using my first name," I yelled down at her as I worked. "Really gives it the ring of sincerity."

They sure made those winching ropes to last. I put my whole body into sawing. Since the winch was still running, I had to follow my original cut up into the bay. For a second, I lost track of Carina, but I could still hear her yelling something. I hacked apart the last few threads.

Both ends of the rope sprung loose, the inside bit snapping against the ceiling. Dax and I were lucky not to lose an eye.

I lunged for the strap hanging from the ceiling, grabbed it, and leaned out.

The look of shock on Carina's face as she fell was damn sure real. Her plan had fallen apart, unraveled like a slipknot. She wheeled her arms and kicked her legs as if she could flail herself into the bay.

"Almost got me, Carina," I yelled, shooting her a wink and a finger gun. "The only person who can catch me is me, but you sure gave it a good run."

Just before Carina hit the canopy, she did what I would've done if I had miscalculated badly enough to be in her boots. She pointed her knuckgun at me.

But she didn't pull the trigger.

A second later, she crashed through the treetops and disappeared.

The black SecOps chopper descended on the clearing where Carina and I had been picked up less than three minutes ago.

I sat down, crossed my legs, and slapped the wide-eyed, open-mouthed Dax on the back like an old friend.

"It's okay, I saved us," I told him, shaking the restless energy out of my shoulders and shifting from one side of my butt to the other. "Let's get back to civilization. This hero could use a shower and some real food."

Of course, all of this was before I found out I was dying of the plague and only Carina could save me.

Acknowledgements

Thanks for reading! There's really no point to writing stories if no one's going to read them. I mean, I'm going to write them either way, but it makes me seem less crazy if real people read my stories when I get done with them. What I'm trying to say is thanks for legitimizing this crazy thing I do. You're awesome.

Everything bad that you've read in this book is my doing, but all of the good things can be attributed to a list of people, muties, and one-pluses from across the pre-Revived Earth who will now be thanked whether they like it or not:

God, Jesus, and the Holy Spirit, who know everything.

The Poet Greene, the Poet Khuri, and the Poet Edison, who all know what they did.

DJ Bodden, who knows how helicopters, throwing knives, and fancy hotels work.

James Hunter, who knows how flame spirits work.

Tim McBain, who knows how serial killers work.

My Joshua, who knows how I work.

And Casey. Wish you were here.

About the Author

I am invincible. I am a mutant. I have 3 hearts and was born with no eyes. I had eyes implanted later. I didn't have hands, either, just stumps. When my eyes were implanted they asked if I would like hands as well and I said, "Yes, I'll take those," and pointed with my stump. But sometimes I'm a hellbender peeking out from under a rock. When it rains, I live in a music box.

But I'm also a tattoo-addict, coffee-junkie, drummer, and aspiring skateboarder. I love you. Let's be friends.

Hang out with me on Goodreads

Drop me a line: imedenhudson@gmail.com

Take a look behind the curtain:
WhiteTrashCappuccino.com

Books, Mailing List, and Reviews

Finishing a good book sucks. It's over. Now what?

Well, if you want to be the first to know when Jubal Van Zandt and the Beautiful Corpse comes out check out www.WhiteTrashCappuccino.com

If you loved or hated this book, you can help keep Jubal in business—or try to put him out of it—by leaving a short, honest review at either Amazon or Goodreads. A sentence or two from you can make all the difference in the world! Thank you in advance.

Other Works by eden Hudson

If you enjoyed Revenge of the Bloodslinger, you might also enjoy eden Hudson's other works, such as the Redneck Apocaplyse series, or you can grab Jubal Van Zandt Book 2, Beautiful Corpse, now!

Revenge of the Bloodslinger: A Jubal Van Zandt Novel

Beautiful Corpse: A Jubal Van Zandt Novel (Book 2)

Soul Jar: A Jubal Van Zandt Novel (Book 3)

Garden of Time: A Jubal Van Zandt Novel (Book 4)

☰

Halo Bound (Redneck Apocalypse Book 1)

Lion's Den (Redneck Apocalypse Book 1.5)

Hell Bent (Redneck Apocalypse Book 2)

God Killer (Redneck Apocalypse Book 3)

Made in the USA
Columbia, SC
25 June 2021